Please Return to

HOLLY HOUSE

CENTER FOR INTEGRATED HEALTHCARE

Annie Huidekoper
Client Relations

Saint Anthony Park Bank Building
2265 Como Avenue • Suite #202 • Saint Paul, MN 55108
(651) 645-6951 • Fax: (651) 645-6961

SHELTER

SHELTER
A COLD WAR MEMORY

a novel by
Peter Huidekoper

Shippen Press
2395 S. Milwaukee St.
Denver, Colorado 80210-5511

Copyright ©1998 by Peter Huidekoper. Printed and bound in the United States of America. All rights reserved. No part of this book may be reproduced or transmitted in any form without permission in writing from the publisher, except where permitted by law. For information, please contact Shippen Press, 2395 S. Milwaukee St., Denver, CO 80210-5511. First printing 1997.

Cover design by Bruce Holdeman, 601 Design, Inc. (Front cover adapted from a drawing by Kimmy Bloomer)
Typography and design by Rudy Garcia.

This book is a work of fiction. The international and national events in *Shelter* are a matter of history and public record. Many of the scenes were created around historical incidents for the purpose of fiction. The author has tried to remain faithful to the flow of public events leading up to October 1962, and to the facts as they were presented to the public during the Cuban Missile Crisis. With the exception of those public figures mentioned by name, such as Kennedy, Khrushchev, Rusk, McNamara, and others, all characters are the complete creation of the author and entirely fictional. Scenes between public figures and these fictional characters are of course invented. Any resemblance of the imaginary characters to actual persons living or dead is unintended and entirely coincidental.

Sherry
Words and Music by Bob Gaudio
© 1962, 1963 (Renewed) Claridge Music Company, A Division of MPL Communications, Inc.
All Rights Reserved

Preassigned Library of Congress Card Number: 97-091082
ISBN: 0-9660861-0-4

Many books, magazines, and newspapers were important to me in my research, above all *The New York Times*, Robert Kennedy's *Thirteen Days – A Memoir of the Cuban Missile Crisis*, and Theodore Sorenson's *Kennedy*. I owe a great deal to John Hersey's *Hiroshima*. I send my special thanks to those who have read and provided useful comment on all or parts of this book, in various drafts, including Tim Brookes, Ruth Byrne, Keith Gaylord, Lisa Gegenschatz, David and Frances Hawkins, Ben McDonald, Ben Nyberg, Mike Pearson, Lisa Schmid, Thordis Simonsen, and members of my family. Thanks also to a number of former students and colleagues who heard selections from this story and encouraged me to continue. – PH

For my parents

"My fellow citizens, let no one doubt that this is a difficult and dangerous effort on which we have set out. No one can foresee precisely what course it will take or what costs or casualties will be incurred.... But the greatest danger of all would be to do nothing."

President Kennedy
from his address to the nation, October 22, 1962

"The crisis had officially begun. Some Americans reacted with panic, most with pride.... Some Americans sought to flee, to hide or to resupply their fallout shelters. The stock market dropped. But by a ratio of ten to one the telegrams received at the White House expressed confidence and support."

Theodore Sorenson
Kennedy

"The possibility of the destruction of mankind was always on his (President Kennedy's) mind. Someone once said that World War III would be fought with atomic weapons and the next war with sticks and stones."

Robert Kennedy
Thirteen Days, A Memoir of the Cuban Missile Crisis

"The world was faced with what many of us felt then, and what since has generally been agreed, was the greatest danger of a catastrophic war since the advent of the nuclear age."

Robert McNamara
from his introduction to *Thirteen Days*

"The world was hanging by a thread, on the edge of death, at the edge of apocalypse."

Alexander Alexeev
Soviet Ambassador to Cuba, 1962

"I see, Mr. President, that you too are not devoid of a sense of anxiety for the fate of the world.... You can be calm in this regard, that we are of sound mind and understand perfectly well that if we attack you, you will respond the same way. But you too will receive the same that you hurl against us. And I think that you also understand this.... This indicates that we are normal people, that we correctly understand and correctly evaluate the situation. Consequently, how can we permit the incorrect actions which you ascribe to us? Only lunatics or suicides, who themselves want to perish and to destroy the whole world before they die, could do this.... If people do not show wisdom, then in the final analysis they will come to a clash, like blind moles, and then reciprocal extermination will begin."

Nikita Khrushchev
from his letter to President Kennedy, October 26, 1962

"Do you think the people in that room realize that if we make a mistake there may be two hundred million dead?"

President Kennedy to his press secretary, Pierre Salinger,
October 26, 1962,
speaking about the Executive Committee of the National Security Council.
The Crisis Years, Kennedy and Khrushchev, 1960-1963, Michael R. Beschloss

"The Cuban missile crisis was a seminal event. History offers no parallel to those thirteen days of October 1962 when the United States and the Soviet Union paused at the nuclear precipice. Never before had there been such a high probability that so many lives would end suddenly. Had war come, it could have meant the death of 100 million Americans, more than 100 million Russians, as well as millions of Europeans. Beside it, the natural calamities and inhumanities of earlier history would have faded into insignificance. Given the odds on disaster which President Kennedy estimated as 'between one out of three and even' — our escape seems awesome."

Graham T. Allison
Essence of Decision

"... At a red light I saw that I was on an Evacuation Route. It took some time for that to penetrate. My head was spinning. I had lost all sense of direction. But the signs — 'Evacuation Route' — continued. Of course, it is the planned escape route from the bomb that hasn't been dropped ... an escape route, a road designed by fear."

John Steinbeck
Travels with Charley, 1962

"Did Khrushchev weigh the importance of the earth and the human species when he sent into Cuba missiles capable of carrying nuclear warheads? And did Kennedy weigh the importance of those things when he blockaded Cuba and then, according to his brother, waited to find out whether events over which 'he no longer had control' would lead the world into a holocaust?"

"Extinction being in its nature outside human experience, is invisible, but we, by rebelling against it, can indirectly make it visible. No one will ever witness extinction, so we must bear witness to it before the fact."

Jonathan Schell
The Fate of the Earth

PROLOGUE

FOR THOSE OF US IN SCHOOL in the early 1960's, the assassination of President John F. Kennedy is the event we remember most clearly. How well I remember it. Friday afternoon. Eighth grade. We remember much of that entire weekend.

Sometimes we say our childhood ended then. Or that the darker side of the '60's began that day, November 22, 1963.

Perhaps.

For me, though, and for many of us, what took place the year before, in late October, was even more painful, and far more enduring in its impact. The Cuban Missile Crisis.

We saw no horrible events that October. There were no images of death, of bloodshed, of grief; no faces that we kept staring at, on the TV — like those of Mrs. Kennedy and the children; no funerals, no horse drawn casket, no world leaders walking through the streets of Washington on the way to Arlington Cemetery; no Lee Harvey Oswalds or Jack Rubys. For those of us in school, there weren't as many tears.

In fact, little happened. Much of the drama took place in our heads, in our imagination — in imagining what if ... what might be.

It was that week when we were told to prepare for the possibility of a nuclear war. Kennedy and Khrushchev spoke boldly, and threatened to use nuclear weapons, weapons that could have killed hundreds of millions, that could have threatened life on earth in ways scientists are still trying to determine.

Of course at age 12 there was much we did not grasp. But even with our limited understanding, we had a glimpse of the truth. We knew enough to tremble, and to wonder.

Now, after all these years, it is still a week we hope to understand.

But we were just kids, some will say. How much could we have known about the complexities of U.S.-Soviet relations and the Cold War, about containment, about anxiety over Cuba — "only ninety miles from our shore," as Kennedy often put it during the 1960 campaign — and a thorn in the side of the United States since Castro came to power in 1959? Kids at 11 or 12 or 13 were too young to understand — weren't they?

We forget, don't we. We forget what our own lives should tell us: how much — to the surprise of many of the adults around us — how much we absorb, as children, how much we hold onto, and keep inside.

Many of us were not as oblivious as adults may have thought, or wished us to be, that fall of 1962. Perhaps we were less dishonest than our parents and teachers and our leaders, less inclined to miss the point as we saw it. We were being told, were led to believe, that our time was nearly up, and that the bombs would soon fly. Wasn't that what we heard?

I know that many of my classmates there in our little town of Riverdale, Connecticut, especially those in my Social Studies class, had more than a vague idea of what was taking place. Mr. Reynolds, our Social Studies teacher, spoke of his pride that we were so well informed, so well prepared, compared to most seventh graders. And talking about that week with people my age, as I have often done, it is clear to me that many of us knew we were not just involved in some strange game of "duck and cover."

I, Tom Chapman, became especially curious about the events of that fall because of my family. My father grew up with politics in Washington, D.C. His father had been friends with Franklin Roosevelt when they were young. By the time FDR became President, however, political differences kept them apart. My uncle, David Chapman, worked for the State Department; he had known "Jack" Kennedy since boarding school days. My father's sister, Aunt Liz, was married to a diplomat. She and her husband were living in Brussels in

1962, but they also had a home in the capital. My father was the only one of the three children not to stay in Washington.

But strong feelings about politics were in the blood. Although my father had gone into business, commuting into New York City as a salesman for a large mineral company, he had majored in history at Dartmouth and always maintained a keen interest in government. Most of the books he read were histories and biographies. One of the two bookcases in the oak-paneled library included Churchill's ten-volume history of World War II. I often saw one of those red-covered books beside my father's chair. Politics was often the main subject when my aunt and uncle visited, or when they came over for drinks at our summer house on Buzzards Bay in Massachusetts. By age ten or eleven, I loved to listen in, to soak up what I could of their conversations — until I felt either lost or restless, and took off for the ball field or the tennis court, or went out for a sail.

It was my father who called my older sister, Lynn, and me into my parents' bedroom to watch Kennedy's inauguration on January 20, 1961. My sister was eleven then, I was ten. My father said something like: "Lynn, Tommy, Mr. Kennedy's presidency may be very important in your lives. I think you should see it begin."

I loved it. President Eisenhower was giving way to this stronger, younger man — at 43, only nine years older than my father. Kennedy's hair blew in the chilly breeze. The conviction in his voice carried across that huge crowd. He and Mrs. Kennedy looked so confident. We had only known Ike in the White House, but how natural, it seemed, that here was our new President. Robert Frost, frail and old, tried to keep his verse from flying away. And then there was Caroline, at three only a year younger than my little brother

Danny, and the baby, "John-John," moving into the White House. I loved all of it. When I saw *Life* magazine offer a special *Inauguration Day Issue* a few weeks later for one dollar, I sent away for it. I looked at the pictures for several days, and then put the magazine in my pile of *Sport* magazines.

And over the next two years, if my mother had the TV on, I sometimes watched ten minutes or so of the President's 4 p.m. press conferences. True, I understood very little of what was said. I liked it, though, when President Kennedy could make the reporters laugh, and seemed unable to hide that wonderful smile, and smoothed his tie with his left hand and turned and pointed with his right hand and took the next question.

What else may have readied me, in one sense at least, for the Cuban Missile Crisis? Civil defense, for one thing. After the failure of the Bay of Pigs invasion in April of 1961, and as tension over Berlin increased that summer, there were several neighbors who installed bomb shelters.

Our next-door neighbors, the Mills, bought one and left it above ground. Randy Mills was two years older than me. Many of the guys in the neighborhood went over to his yard to play softball that spring. The field was narrow: anything hit well to left field was over the stone wall and out onto the road; and a ball hit to right would go behind a row of pine trees. The Mills placed their shelter amid the pine trees. There was no brush in the way, and the first branch on the closest pine tree was ten feet off the ground, so sometimes a line drive would ricochet off that bomb shelter and shoot back into short right. I hit lefty sometimes — my father had taught me to switch hit, like my favorite player, Mickey Mantle — and when I connected well and banged one off the shelter I had to hustle for a double.

The presence of the shelter led to jokes about "bombing one out there" whenever we drove one between the two nearby pines in the direction of that ugly metal frame. And if the game became one-sided, someone would tell the losers they might want "to surrender," "take shelter," or "to go hide from our lethal attack" — and point out to right field.

Randy took me inside the shelter once. It was nearly bare. There was a "toilet" — made of wood. I saw two six-packs of Coca-Cola, ten cans of soup, a jug of water, comic books, three pillows, and a sleeping bag. Randy told me their shelter was made differently than some others; the walls were so thick, he said, it did not need to be buried. I didn't really understand. All I knew was it was for hiding out during a war, and protection against "radioactive fallout," which I was told was a kind of deadly poison.

When we played war, or spotted a military plane high overhead, it was still the Japs and the Nazis who were usually the bad guys. But in the early 1960's most of us knew that it was Khrushchev and the Russians who would be on the other side of a real war. Few of us knew what Khrushchev and the Communists believed in, but we were pretty clear it was the opposite of what we believed in. We all knew Khrushchev's line, "I will bury you." I heard my uncle speak of him as "scary," as "a fool," and sometimes simply as "a bastard" — a word that always drew my attention, ever since my parents sent me to my room for trying it once, at age nine.

It was Khrushchev's visit to the United States in the fall of 1960 that helped me see that he was a dangerous man. I had watched the TV news with my parents, and had seen him pound his shoe on the table in the United Nations. I was amazed. At school a few of the guys made fun of him. Some of the sixth graders that week, sitting together in the cafeteria over lunch, took off their sneakers and pounded them on the table and waved their arms and acted as if they had lost their minds. They had to stop, though, when one of the teachers came over and told them to knock it off and put their sneakers back on their feet, where they belonged.

There were other events during the year leading up to the fall of 1962 that may suggest why, more so than many of my classmates, I was intrigued by, prepared for, or vulnerable to the events that took place that October. But I repeat, I was hardly alone. Many of us cannot forget that week, and those drills, and all our talk, however ignorant or comical or irrational, about Khrushchev and bomb shelters and war. We knew enough, when the blockade began, with the Soviet missiles still crossing the Atlantic towards Cuba, to believe there was good reason to fear that this was it, to believe that — in spite of the comforting words from adults, it was not going to be OK. Life was going to end, quite suddenly, before we had a chance to live. It should not surprise anyone that some of us have been so fixed on that autumn. And why some of us need to try to recall the moments of those weeks in some detail, to try to communicate some of the anxiety — the quiet panic and unspoken dread that we knew.

And there is another motive for this look back, this Cold War memory.

Prologue

My generation had the first child's eye view of what the doctrine of mutual assured destruction — MAD — might be all about. And Kennedy and Khrushchev were compelled, as few other leaders have been, to face the terror of nuclear holocaust. But what did we learn? How were we changed? Do we understand what it meant?

My fear stayed with me, for much too long. In too many ways, you see, I stayed down in the bomb shelter in our back yard and continued to anticipate the day when World War III would begin. The fear has left its mark. Some used to say that no one had been hurt by nuclear weapons since August 9, 1945, when we dropped that plutonium bomb over Nagasaki. We know better now. The effect of the nuclear weapons tests on many in Nevada, Utah, and Arizona is perhaps the most tangible evidence. But my own life tells me that the damage — far less horrible and deadly — has been real in other ways, too.

I can believe in a future now. Maybe for this reason I can finally write about that autumn as something past, a time when I felt shaken, and silenced.

Now I can find my voice, and remember what it was we were asked to believe, what growing up in the nuclear age was like for me, and for others.

I remember, in the hope that I will put my old fear behind me.

And I remember, in the hope that generations to follow will not know the same fear.

"And now a force was in hand how much more strong, and we hadn't had time to develop the means to think, for man has to have feelings and then words before he can come close to thought and, in the past at least, that has taken a long time."

John Steinbeck
Travels with Charley, 1962

CHAPTER ONE

July 1961–August 1962

THERE WERE FOUR OF US — Lynn, me, my younger sister, Beth, and Danny. My mother and father seldom argued in front of us, but in late July, not long after the Mills had bought their bomb shelter, we heard our parents exchange sharp words about buying a shelter. My mother thought it was a good idea. A hardware store next to Riverdale's A & P put a silver-gray bomb shelter in the middle of their parking lot, on an island flanked by two pine trees. One afternoon I went down to the A & P with my mother; after I helped bring out the groceries, she asked me to come take a look.

We went inside the shelter. It was dark. I was surprised to see how totally empty it was. Just four walls. That night, several minutes after we had all been called down for supper, my parents brought the argument into the kitchen.

"I'd just feel a little more secure, Andy, that's all," my mother said, coming in just after my father.

"Sarah, it's not going to happen," he snapped. He had his martini in his right hand. "This is panic, it's hysteria — it'll go away. We don't have to step in line." He took another sip — his glass was nearly empty — as he moved closer to the sink. "It'll just be two thousand dollars down the drain," he added, lifting up his martini and pouring out what remained in the glass: "—like this."

"I just want to make sure we have done all we can—"

My father put the glass down with a loud "clink!" and turned around. He raised his voice loud enough to make me shake. "Not this way, Sarah! It's nonsense!" Then he grew quieter, but his jaws remained tight, his breath whistled through his nose, and his blue eyes glared. "Dammit, let's end this." He looked around at the four of us, and then added, "Please."

Sometimes Danny and I could hear their fights. Our room was right beside theirs. Lying in our beds, we could hear when they raised their voices a few feet away from us. Usually the words were muffled; the walls in that big old stone house were strong. But twice that week the quarrel was loud and clear. The second time both Lynn and Beth came into our room, crying. I closed my door behind them, and we listened. "Why don't they stop?" Lynn asked, still sobbing.

A few days later we left for our month in Sandy Harbor. As he had always done, my father came up only on weekends during August, before taking the last week off for a vacation. It was then that I heard Uncle David describe what was taking place in Berlin.

My uncle had joined Vice-President Johnson on his trip to Germany after the Berlin Wall went up on August 13. In Sandy Harbor, over drinks on Labor Day weekend, he told my parents what he had seen. They sat in a circle, in front of our summer house, and I listened in. It sounded very dramatic, even though I knew little of what this was all about. I could see that my uncle was upset with President Kennedy.

I sat just outside their circle, reading the sports pages of *The New York Times*. I was trying to see if Mickey Mantle still had a chance to beat Babe Ruth's home run record. It disappointed me to see that Number Seven was beginning to fall behind Ruth's pace, while his teammate, Roger Maris, might make it. If anyone deserved to break the record, I thought it was Mickey.

"I still think Khrushchev got the better of us in Vienna," my uncle said, "and he's confident he can push, push, push. Test us, scare us a bit, see if we crack. Find out if Jack will give in some more."

"But this talk of war," my father said, "all this hysteria about civil defense, isn't this exaggerating the situation?"

"Bullshit," my uncle barked, and I looked up. "We're not going to sell out Berlin. God, I hope not anyway. Andy, you wouldn't believe the shelters they have ready for us at State. I wouldn't call it hysteria."

I saw my parents catch each other's eyes for a second, but my father looked away.

In September, 1961, I entered sixth grade. It was thanks to our teacher, Mrs. Schwartz, and not just my family, that I began to follow the news more closely that year. We studied the Greeks for several months, and Mrs. Schwartz called us her "Athenians," as she wanted us to grow up to be "good citizens, men and women who want to participate in your government." We liked Mrs. Schwartz. We considered ourselves the top group of the four sixth-grade classes there at West Elementary School. None of the other three classes had as much homework, we were quite sure of that. We felt we deserved her.

Mrs. Schwartz grew teary-eyed the third week of school when she told us about the death of the Secretary-General of the United Nations, Dag Hammarskjold. That winter, when all the sixth graders were bussed into New York City on a field trip, we went into the Metropolitan Museum in the morning with the other classes. But in the afternoon, when everyone else went to the zoo in Central Park, Mrs. Schwartz took our class for a tour of the U.N.

We spent more time on history and social studies in sixth grade than I ever had before. I remember cutting out several stories from *Junior Scholastics*, which we were given biweekly at school, *The New York Times*, our daily paper at home, and *U.S. News and World Report*, one of the magazines my parents received, for a report on the countries of Southeast Asia and the fighting there. I learned that the Communists were trying to move into that part of the world, as well as some countries in Africa.

My father fell ill in February and March. At first the doctors said it was a bad flu, and then they said he was very tired. By April he was at Cedar Grove. My mother said it was a hospital. "Your father needs the rest, that's where the doctors want him to be," she explained.

I missed him very much that spring, especially as it was baseball season. He had always been my coach. When I was eight and nine, in Cub League, he coached our Saturday morning games; when I was ten, he became my Little League coach with the Tigers. That first year, and the year after, he had left the city early twice a week for our 6 p.m. games, getting there by 5:15, pitching batting practice to us with his tie still on. But in the spring of 1962, for the first six weeks of the season, in my last year of Little League, he never saw me play.

In May we were asked to do our biggest report of the year — "your final project before junior high school," Mrs. Schwartz said, "and I hope your best." I chose to do mine on President Kennedy.

I pulled out my *Inauguration Day Issue* of *Life* and read his speech. I liked it. I did my report on both his life and on his Inaugural Address. I enjoyed reading about his school days, and finding out what a hero he had been in World War II after his PT-109 was destroyed. It reminded me of the story in our book on Greek heroes, about Odysseus, surviving his shipwreck, conquering exhaustion, battling the odds. I loved knowing that my President had done that, too. I tried to read some of *Profiles of Courage, a Young Reader's*

Edition, which my mother gave me on my twelfth birthday, May 16, but I found it too hard.

We had to give oral reports as well as a written report. Some of the passages in the President's speech were difficult, and I asked my mother for help. She went over it with me line by line for two or three nights, between eight and nine o'clock, after she had put both Beth and Danny to bed. She encouraged me to quote President Kennedy's words often. By the day of my oral report I had three or four points to make.

I gave my report on May 29 — President Kennedy's birthday. I spoke of "the hope and promise" in the President's Inaugural Address. "America, he said, would lead the world in a crusade for freedom. He believes that our nation has the courage to do anything 'to assure the survival and the success of liberty.'"

"He spoke to 'friend and foe alike,'" I quoted, "to every nation 'whether it wishes us well or ill,' even 'to those nations who would make of themselves our adversaries.' America, he said, had been 'granted the role of defending freedom in its maximum hour of danger' — and he promised we would do everything to carry out this great task."

When I finished Mrs. Schwartz complimented me: "Very nicely done, Tommy." Then she spoke for several minutes about how Kennedy's election had been a wonderful event for all young people in America. "The idealism and energy of the new President has excited the youth of this country," she said, "and has made them feel more important once again — and more patriotic."

There were three passages in the Inaugural Address that I had not used. I did not understand them. They were dark, and suggested the possibility of something awful. They did not seem to fit in with the hopeful tone of Kennedy's speech. When I asked my mother about them she just said they were a warning "about what could happen," and left it at that.

The first passage read:

> Man holds in his mortal hands the power to abolish all forms of human poverty — and all forms of human life.

The second one, more confusing than the first, read:

> Both sides (must) begin the quest for peace before the dark powers of destruction unleashed by science engulf all humanity in planned or accidental self-destruction. So let us begin anew.

And the third:

> But neither can two great and powerful groups of nations take comfort from our present course ... both rightly alarmed by the steady spread of the deadly atom, yet both racing to alter that uncertain balance of terror that stays the hand of mankind's final war.

Those passages were not clear to me in May, 1962. They would mean much more to me in October, during the missile crisis, when I pulled out President Kennedy's speech again.

That spring I learned a lot about bomb shelters from my friend, Ian Gilbert, who was also in Mrs. Schwartz's class. Ian lived on Woodside Lane, just off Bayberry Hill. When I looked out my room at night I could see the light from his house through the pine trees, those two acres of pines where he and I had spent many afternoons, creating forts, playing tag, and trying to build camp fires. After our fifth grade teacher read *The Adventures of Tom Sawyer* to us, a chapter every morning for a month, we sometimes pretended we were Tom and Huck. We had been friends since he and his family arrived in Riverdale, back in second grade. He was not like my other friends at school. He was two or three inches taller than I was, thin, and not very good at sports. He often seemed lazy in school, but he loved to read. The rest of us laughed when he was caught reading a novel (among them that year, *Animal Farm*, *The Count of Monte Cristo*, and *Connecticut Yankee in King Arthur's Court*) while we were doing arithmetic or mythology or writing. But he and I got along well. I admired how bright he was, and envied his boldness.

Ian could question Mrs. Schwartz or calmly argue with her. He was never impolite; he seemed to make Mrs. Schwartz think. His parents were much older than mine; he had a brother in college and a sister about to graduate from high school. Ian's father made me nervous. He was a physics professor, a serious man who stayed in his study a lot and never came out to play with us on weekends. But Mrs. Gilbert was very friendly. That spring I spent a number of Saturday nights at the Gilberts.

Ian did his report for school on shelters. His father said they were not safe. Ian told me he couldn't prove that in five or six pages, so he described what they were supposed to do.

He used a *Life* magazine article for much of his report, and he carried it with him to and from school for over a week. The cover of the magazine had a creepy picture of a man in a strange plastic suit; the words below the photograph called it a **"CIVILIAN FALLOUT SUIT."** John Glenn and Alan Shepherd had looked almost normal in their space suits compared to this strange outfit. Along the right-hand side of the cover stood these headlines, which I had memorized after a week of sharing morning bus rides with Ian:

HOW YOU CAN SURVIVE FALLOUT

97 out of 100 people can be saved ...
Detail plans for building shelter ...

AND A LETTER TO YOU FROM PRESIDENT KENNEDY

I looked through the magazine a couple of times on the bus, and read some of President Kennedy's letter. I stared at the picture of a family packed together inside one small room for weeks, the caption said, maybe months. It made me think of Tom and Becky trapped in the cave.

I knew my father thought all of this was nonsense. I was sure he was right. But someone else was talking to me that April and May about the end of the world, telling stories that felt both more important — and terribly real.

Kaarlo Saarinen, my sixth-grade Sunday School teacher at the First Presbyterian Church, had asked us to read many chapters from John and Matthew that year. Unlike my previous Sunday School teachers, Mr. Saarinen clearly wanted us to think hard about the Bible, and what Jesus said, and what it meant to believe in Him. But ever since Easter Mr. Saarinen often spoke of Christ's return. I began to fear Judgment Day, imagining Christ was on his way when we had our four or five thunderstorms at night that spring. When they came I would lie awake, sometimes going over to lift up the shade and look out, studying the various streaks of lightning, or looking down as the cars and the front yard all appeared in the flash of light. After such storms it took me another hour or so to get to sleep. If He wasn't coming now, I wondered, when *would* He come?

During one of those storms I went into my mother's room, in tears, and told her what I was afraid of. I tried to tell her how I thought it would happen — the thunder would announce He was here, we would look up and see Him on a cloud, the lightning would flash around Him ... — it seemed close to what Mr. Saarinen, or the Bible, had taught us. My mother tried to console me. She didn't fault Mr. Saarinen, but she did say, "You don't need to take everything so literally, Tommy."

My father came back from the hospital shortly after the Memorial Day weekend. His first night back he called me down into the library and asked me to explain what Mr. Saarinen was teaching us. I did not want to complain; I tried to show how much I liked Mr. Saarinen and how much I was learning. But after I answered, my father threatened to take me out of the last three weeks of class. "I can see it," he said to my mother, bitterly, "Kaarlo must love to have these kids wrapped around his little finger." He called up my teacher, with me right there, and told him "to stop trying to scare the hell out of these kids." I was embarrassed, and a little angry. I felt very uncomfortable when I walked into Mr. Saarinen's class the next Sunday morning.

In mid-June my parents told me it seemed "the right time" for me to go off to the tennis camp we had discussed for a couple of years. "New people, all that tennis, doing some camping, it ought to be fun," my mother said. "It will be good to be more independent," my father told me. He had left his job in New York City and was looking for work — perhaps a company he could buy. "Besides," he added, "I won't be around much anyway."

Those three weeks in July of 1962 up in the mountains of Vermont, just north of Stowe, were the first time I was away from home for more than a night or two. The thunderstorms there proved even scarier, nearly lifting our little cabins off the ground. It took me years before I no longer looked up when lightning flashed, wondering if this time Christ would appear.

I joined my family in Buzzards Bay the last weekend of July. August passed, and it was almost time to go back to Riverdale and begin seventh grade. But we still had Labor Day weekend, and the final tennis tournament, and our last dinner with our grandmother and cousins. Only later did I realize events were already taking place, events hinted at that weekend, that would to lead to the missile crisis in October.

"The hydrogen bomb is a greater evil than any evil it is intended to meet."
> U Thant, Acting Secretary General of the United Nations
> from a speech given at the University of Warsaw
> on the nuclear test ban treaty
> Quotation of the Day, *The New York Times*
> Sept. 1, 1962

CHAPTER TWO

Labor Day Weekend, 1962

LABOR DAY WEEKEND WAS SUNNY AND WARM, with a good breeze coming in from the south. My father only took those three days off that year, so there was no cruise over to Wood's Hole and Martha's Vineyard and Nantucket. In July he had bought out one of the three owners of a sports store in Riverdale, and he became president of the company. He made the four-and-a-half hour drive to Sandy Harbor on Friday night. On Saturday morning, the first of September, we played golf and went for a sail in the widgeon. At 2 p.m. Uncle David and my father played in the finals of the Men's

Doubles, which they had won five out of the last six years. That Saturday much of Sandy Harbor gathered at the casino, in front of court number one, to watch them play.

I sat beside my grandmother, enjoying her familiar Yardley lavender perfume, there under the casino roof. She kept her wide straw hat on her head. Earlier that summer, while at tennis camp, we watched old films of the finals at Wimbledon, with the Queen of England looking on. My grandmother, I thought, sat there much like the Queen herself.

"You'll be playing with your father in this tournament in a few years," Nana said softly as she bent my way. "Andy and David have another couple of tournaments — then it will be Andy and *Tommy* Chapman." She smiled. "I look forward to it."

That would be strange, I thought, to play with my father, to take my uncle's place. I expected to watch them play in the finals of the Men's Doubles for many years to come.

But I had little problem thinking about my future, there at twelve, before the events of that fall. I could imagine being a professional baseball player, or an astronomer, or an archaeologist — or a businessman, like my father.

I had known little about my father's job in New York City. But sometimes he had traveled out west, or to Japan, or South Africa. I was glad to think he would no longer be away for so long.

I was especially glad to see him healthy again. He was playing as well as ever. He raced back for lobs and crashed into the back screen as he had always done, and he slammed several overheads with enough force to send the ball bouncing out over the back fence. He and Uncle David won in straight sets, 6-4, 6-2. They came home, and my father changed and took a swim out in front of the house, and Uncle David and Aunt Carol walked over and joined him. Our cottage was one hundred feet from the sea wall overlooking the bay. Uncle David's house stood by the road that came down to the water, about four hundred feet from us, and was situated a little further from the sea wall. Nana's big house was at the top of the gentle rise. In the middle of the four acres was our baseball field, with a large new backstop. Center field, I had figured, was exactly half way up the hill in the two-and-a-half-minute run to Nana's house.

My parents and my aunt and uncle then brought their gin and tonics out to the lounge chairs in front of the house. They sat around the makeshift table — an old lobster pot I had found washed up in the rocks, with the net still inside, now covered with a piece of glass. Three large shells served as ashtrays. My mother and Aunt Carol brought out the peanuts, crackers, and dip. I had already made my own milkshake — Coke, coffee ice cream, milk, and a few pieces of ice, thrown into the blender for ninety seconds — and watched the end of the Red Sox game.

Boston beat Minnesota in the ninth, 5-4. The announcers gave the Yankees' score, too; Ralph Terry had won his twentieth for New York, stretching their lead over the Twins to four games. In summing up the Yankees' game the announcers mentioned no home runs. Mickey had 398 homers; maybe I could see number 400 when we returned to Riverdale, on channel 11. I looked for *The New York Times*, which my mother had bought that morning, and took it outside to join the adults.

My father and Uncle David finished reviewing the match, and then all four of them discussed my father's new company. My mother said, "I think we'll see more of Andy, eventually." My father said he was happy to be involved in something more fun than minerals, and even happier if he never saw New York City again. And he spoke of "opportunities for growth," "possible branches in Stamford and Greenwich...."

I listened, and studied the way all four of them held their cigarettes, and leafed through the second section of the paper until I found the sports pages. I checked the American League statistics: Mickey was second in the league in hitting. He had suffered another bad injury that year, causing him to miss 40 games. It happened on May 18: I remembered because it was two days after I turned twelve. I had read the next day how he had "gone down as if he had been shot" as he tried to beat out a groundball, with two outs in the ninth and the tying run on base. I had often read of Mickey's courage, playing in pain on two bad legs. But he was fairly healthy now and having another good year. If he finished with enough official at bats he could still win the batting title. In the National League the Dodgers were being chased by the Giants. It would be great, I thought, if the Giants won, and both Mickey and Willie Mays were in the World Series.

The adults' conversation had turned to the Berlin Wall, and the story of Peter Fechter, the 18-year-old who had recently tried to climb over the wall and had been shot by the East German soldiers. I had seen the grim pictures in *Life*.

I finished the sports pages and folded section two back to its first page. I glanced at the Quote of the Day, by U Thant. It meant little to me, although it made me think of Riverdale, and Ian, and his report on bomb shelters. Then I put section two under the front of the paper and rested the *Times* on my knees. My mother passed the peanuts around.

I took a large handful and put them down on the paper. I noticed that they partly covered a map of Cuba and Florida and the Bahamas there on the front page. As I picked up the peanuts, three or four at a time, the headline over the map became clearer:

Boats Off Cuba Fire at U.S. Navy Plane; Havana Cautioned

"And what is Washington up to, Dave?" my father asked my uncle. "Where are you moving on this? Khrushchev can't prolong this Berlin thing forever, can he?"

"I talked with Rusk about this yesterday and gave him my recommendations, but I don't know how much the President is listening to State right now." He took a sip of his drink, before adding: "He'd much sooner listen to Bobby or McNamara."

I looked at him, and at my Dad. My father, with sandy blond hair, sat straight up. Uncle David, with darker hair, now turning ever more gray, was leaning back. He slumped down enough to make himself look shorter than my father, although in fact he was two or three inches taller. My uncle was heavier, as well; he rested his drink on the top of his stomach, where there was a considerable bulge, supporting it with his left hand. His cigarette was in his right hand. My father, always lean, had no such pillow. But neither was he as thin, or as pale, as he had looked in the spring.

"Washington *isn't* moving, to answer your question. We're reacting." My uncle took a drag of his Marlboro, and continued. "I gather that Khrushchev will grace us with his presence again this fall. If he meets Jack, I have no doubt he'll probably take advantage of the President again, as he did in Vienna. And then Nikita will visit comrade Castro and give him a great Big Bear hug—"

"Yes, what about this," and I saw my father point to the paper in my lap, "this news about, what was it, 5,000 Soviet specialists are reported to be in Cuba working for Castro? And that Cuba has a general military alert on?"

I felt lost, but wanted to try to hang on a little longer. This was the kind of Washington talk I enjoyed.

My uncle shrugged. "If they think we're planning on another invasion, it's news to me, though I don't know if it would be so wrong."

"Not another Bay of Pigs," Aunt Carol exclaimed, picking at her blond curls, all spongy and tangled. Aunt Carol's hair always looked comical to me after she finished a swim.

"Christ no, the real thing," Uncle David insisted. "We'd be better off doing it now than when they have 10,000 Soviet specialists, and God knows what else." He started to reach my way: "Tommy, could I see that?" I picked up the remaining peanuts and gave him the first section of the paper. "Do you know what we're talking about?" he added, looking at me. "Do you study current events at school?"

"Tommy had an excellent teacher this year," my mother interjected. "He did a terrific report on the President."

"A little, yes," I answered my uncle, hoping he would not ask me about my report. "I know something about the Bay of Pigs. We messed it up, didn't we?"

He laughed. "Your President messed it up, yes, exactly. Messed it up but good." He had opened to the editorial page. "Did you see the editorials this morning?" He was talking to my mother and father again. They shook their heads, no. "The *Times*, of course, wants us to tiptoe away from what's really happening." He read to himself for a second, taking a puff on his cigarette. "Here:

> To counteract the recent developments in Cuba with American arms and lives would demand a much higher price than the situation warrants. It is concededly an ugly, difficult and dangerous state-of-affairs, but not a cause of war. To invade Cuba under present circumstances would — as President Kennedy indicated at his press conference this week — be the course of incredible folly.

That's so much bullshit," my uncle said, tossing the paper onto the table. "We know the Soviets are not just sending the Cubans vodka and caviar. Five-thousand specialists didn't show up just to teach them how to harvest sugar! We have to challenge them."

"Even if it means war?" Aunt Carol asked. "Honey, you can't mean it!"

He nodded, slightly, and tapped the ashes off the end of his cigarette. "If we have to, yes."

I looked out at the bay and the dozens of boats in front of us: two sunfish close to shore, ten or more beetle cats, many sloops, and a few yawls, some carrying their spinnakers as they sailed downwind for the harbor. I studied two of the yawls as they brought down their spinnakers, one smoothly, one dropping her sail into the bay for a few seconds. There were many motor boats as well, including several small fishing boats between our land and the beach two miles to the south.

The breeze wasn't dying, as it sometimes did late in the afternoon. It might be my last chance this year to sail alone. I could go out for an hour and still be back in time to get dressed up for our end-of-summer dinner at Nana's. As I rose to leave, my father picked up everyone's glass to go inside and pour a refill. He said he knew there were several Republican Senators calling for an invasion, but he found it "hard to believe Cuba was worth a major fight." Then I heard my uncle say something about "wishful thinking."

    The twelve-foot widgeon was tied to our mooring thirty yards from the shoreline. I swam on out, raised the sail, and cast off. I tacked into the wind for thirty minutes, towards the beach in Sandy Harbor, and then came back with the wind behind me. I thought about my father's new company. I had always loved The Riverdale Sports Shop. Most of all I loved walking in there every April — up until this past spring — walking in there with my father as we picked out the new bats for the Cub League and Little League teams, Louisville Sluggers, size 28 to size 31. It was there that I had bought my Stan Musial Rawlings baseball glove, my Voit basketball, and my Cary Middlecoff five and seven irons. It was exciting to think that our house would soon be flooded with new footballs and baseballs and tennis rackets.

    Still, it was Uncle David's job that seemed so much more interesting, so important. He could talk of "Jack" and Berlin and war with Cuba, and he could sit down with the Secretary of State to talk about Khrushchev. Maybe when I grew up, I thought, I could work in Washington, too.

    As I brought the widgeon back in, I thought of entering Riverdale Junior High that Wednesday. All the former sixth graders from the three different elementary schools would now be together. We would take five different classes with five different teachers, as my sister Lynn had done the year before. It sounded complicated, and hard. I couldn't wait.

On Monday I drove back with my father in his VW. Lynn, Beth, and Danny went in the Rambler with my mother. I had the papers in the front seat with me so that I could read the sports. But the front page of both Sunday and Monday's papers told of an incredible earthquake in Iran. At least 10,000 were dead. I remembered words from Mr. Saarinen's Sunday School class, of "earthquakes and terrors and great signs" when Christ would return. I put the papers down. A few minutes later, on the edge of South Dartmouth, we passed the estate of the Holy Cross Fathers and the Dominican Sisters, and the huge sign across their front lawn, each letter ten feet high:

GOD LOVES YOU

The sign had always seemed quite odd to me, some kind of strange promise or warning. This year, though, given all I had learned in Sunday School, it seemed a reminder. God loves you, I thought, and you better be ready. I wondered if my father remembered his angry words to Mr. Saarinen in early June. But as we passed the sign and the church and the abbey, my father offered his usual friendly farewell: "Good-bye Fathers, good-bye Sisters! See you next year!"

"The Soviet Union announced tonight that it has agreed to supply arms to Cuba and to provide technical specialists to train Cuban forces."

The New York Times
Sept. 3, 1962

"The Soviet Union's announcement yesterday that it would provide military aid to Cuba to meet threats of 'imperialist' attack raises anew questions of the present meaning and effect of the Monroe Doctrine."

The New York Times
editorial, Sept. 4, 1962

CHAPTER THREE

Back to School

ON WEDNESDAY MORNING, SEPTEMBER 5, Lynn and I walked down Bayberry Hill, past the Mills' house on the right, past Woodside Lane, to the Junior High bus stop at the corner of Chichester and Bayberry. The new schedule said the bus would stop here around 7:35. "Hey, Chapper," some of the guys said, as I arrived. After a summer away, it was nice to hear my nickname again. Immediately I noticed how large some of the eighth graders were. I was surprised to see one of them, Jeff Connors, not even hiding his pack of Lucky Strike cigarettes. He and Josh and Mike had longer hair than the rest of us; their hair was still wet from combing it at home — slicked back. I was glad to see that three of my neighbors, entering seventh grade with me, still wore crewcuts.

At the last minute Ian came running down the hill, just ahead of the yellow bus. Panting hard, he arrived a few seconds after the bus had come to a stop. His forehead was damp; his blond bangs stood up, an uncombed mess. We took a seat together. I had gone over to see him the day before. He, too, was growing much faster than I was. I had to look up to him more than I remembered.

Riverdale Junior High was located near the center of town. The bus took us several blocks away from the train station and all the commuters. The Riverdale station was the end of the line, one of the reasons for the town motto — "The Next Station to Heaven." Near one stop on the way to school we saw the train race by, taking the commuters over to Stamford, and then on into New York City. My father, I realized, would no longer have to board that train every morning.

The Junior High consisted of two old turn-of-the-century brick buildings: the Main Building, as it was simply called, and the Annex. After six years all on one floor at West Elementary School, it was fun to try to adjust to this new schedule, climbing up and down stairs, twice changing buildings as I went from class to class — from homeroom to Social Studies to Math to gym to English in the morning, and then, after lunch, on to French I and Science. I took it as a challenge, during the four-minute passing period, to try to hustle around the large groups of students blocking the hallways or stairways, talking and laughing and passing books and notes and candy. I tried to weave through those crowds unnoticed. Sometimes, though, especially during the first few weeks of school, when I bumped into a pretty girl, I felt embarrassed and happy at the same time. But a couple of the tall eighth-grade girls who looked so much older, so mature — and who also looked down on me — would stare, briefly, as if to say, "Can't you see where you're going little boy?"

My homeroom was in the basement of the Annex, right across the hall from the boys' locker room. The pipes on the ceiling reminded me of our cellar at home. They were quiet early that September, but by late October, when they went to work, their puffing and popping and clinking often interrupted our homeroom teacher's efforts to speak to us.

Twenty-seven of us — a few familiar faces, including Cindy Mellum — sat before Mrs. Brady, our homeroom teacher, that Wednesday morning and listened to instructions about lockers, lunch periods, and cafeteria policy. I was glad to see two girls, Kitty and Pam, who had been in my sixth-grade class with Mrs. Schwartz. They looked great. I wondered if I would be in any of the same classes as Debbie Myers. She had gone to Center Elementary School, but I knew her from the Presbyterian Church. Now I could see her every day. As Mrs. Brady read us a list of rules — no smoking, no fighting, no stealing, no leaving the school grounds before 2:30, among others — I noticed Cindy's ugly, new, blue-rimmed glasses. Poor Cindy, I thought, everything she does for herself makes her seem even more ridiculous.

It was Cindy, as it turned out, who also helped me understand more clearly what was taking place in late October. Cindy and I had been in class together in the fifth and sixth grades. She was brilliant and moody, but strange. Anything could send her into tears. When our sixth-grade class had gathered around the TV in February to watch the lift-off as John Glenn began his three orbits around the earth, we applauded and cheered as we saw the rocket climb ever so slowly into the sky. All of us, that is, except Cindy. She left the room in hysterics, with Mrs. Schwartz right behind her. I didn't snicker with the others, but I couldn't understand it. In May she had been too nervous to get past the first minute of her report in front of the class. We heard she was allowed to do it after school, standing in front of the classroom, with only Mrs. Schwartz as her audience.

My mother and Mrs. Mellum were friends, and ever since fifth grade my mother often reminded me to try to be nice to Cindy. I tried not to be mean, though it was hard not to laugh at her when our class played kickball or dodgeball; she galloped awkwardly when she ran, and many of the guys called her "Goofy" to her face. Even the girls often made fun of her. I remember feeling confused, and sympathetic, the previous spring, while my father was still away at the hospital, when I heard one of the guys mimicking Cindy, and saying, with a sneer, "That girl's crazy enough to go to Cedar Grove."

Before homeroom ended that first morning Mrs. Brady explained the procedure for a fire alarm. She asked two of the taller boys, Jerry and Mike, to be responsible for closing the windows in the back as the rest of us lined up by the door. She asked all of us not to push or run to the door, but to walk, not to get too excited, and never to panic. She asked us to stay together as a group so that she could take attendance in the parking lot.

We had our first fire drill two days later, on Friday morning. Two people pushed over chairs in the rush, but most of us did not hurry, or worry; we knew it was a drill. Mrs. Brady was quiet, but relaxed. She watched us closely and advised us to remain silent and to stay in line as we headed outside. She seemed to enjoy the first drill, even though it went on for nearly fifteen minutes. I found myself looking at her, at her blond hair, at her legs, and her high heels. I had never had a teacher who was so young and beautiful and nice. The night before I said something about her to Lynn, and she laughed and teased me, saying, "half of the eighth-grade boys are in love with her, too." Mrs. Brady took attendance in the parking lot, twenty-seven of us saying "here" or "yes." Other than that we were silent. After a few minutes, though, we began to talk, and she joined in. It was quite warm, even that early in the day. Summer wasn't over yet.

We practiced the fire drill three more times that September. By the end of the month we were told that we had it down to under six minutes.

That fall, before school began, before walking in to homeroom, I often went into the boys' locker room to look in the mirror. My hair was too short to need combing, but I wanted to make sure I looked all right. I wanted to look good for two people — Debbie Myers, and Mrs. Brady.

After a week of homeroom, I noticed that Mrs. Brady was not having us pray. We said the pledge of allegiance, but there was no prayer. In elementary school we had started class with the pledge, and often sang "My Country 'Tis of Thee" or "God Bless America" or "America the Beautiful." Ever since fourth grade we usually said the Lord's Prayer, or Psalm 23 or Psalm 100, from the King James Version. Sometimes Mrs. Schwartz had asked us to close our eyes as she read a few lines from Proverbs, and then said, "And may You bless us and be with us as we begin this new day. Amen."

I saw a copy of *Time* on Mrs. Brady's desk. The drawing on the cover showed a wall, and barbed wire just above it, and two hands — one hand hanging on to the wire, the fingers wrapped around it, the other hand reaching through the wire, onto the near side of the wall, pulling the body up. But I could see no head, and no body. The only words on the cover were **"THE WALL."** I remembered the conversation at Sandy Harbor with my aunt and uncle and my parents. The picture had to be about Peter Fechter.

Time was there in the classroom, and *Paris Match*, but no Bible. I went up to ask Mrs. Brady about this as we were leaving homeroom.

"It's been decided that it's unconstitutional to use prayer in public schools, Tommy. The Supreme Court decided this over the summer."

"Unconstitutional?" I asked, startled. "I don't understand."

"It's complicated, Tommy. Guess we have to say a prayer at home in the morning, right?"

"Yes," I agreed. I wondered what Mr. Saarinen would think of this. My eyes fell again on her copy of *Time*. "Mrs.

Brady, could I borrow that from you when you're done with it?"

"Sure," she said. "Of course."

I hurried upstairs to my first period class, Social Studies, with Mr. Reynolds. It was his class, that first week, as well as what I had heard from Uncle David, that fostered so much curiosity about Berlin.

And it was his class those next seven weeks — along with all that Cindy would help me see, and all that I had learned from my father, from my uncle, from Mrs. Schwartz, and from Ian — that gave me that much more awareness of what was happening once the President spoke to the nation on October 22, and let us know of the missiles in Cuba, of the American blockade of that island, and *something* of the dangers, the risks, before us.

"There is no evidence of any organized combat force in Cuba from any Soviet bloc country; of military bases provided to Russia; of a violation of the 1934 treaty relating to Guantanamo; of the presence of offensive ground-to-ground missiles; or of other significant capability either in Cuban hands or under Soviet direction and guidance.

"Were it to be otherwise, the gravest issues would arise."

from President Kennedy's statement on Cuba
Sept. 4, 1962

CHAPTER FOUR

Mr. Reynolds

LYNN HAD WARNED ME about Mr. Reynolds. He had not been her teacher the year before, but when I showed her my schedule, with his name on it, "Per.1/Social Studies/ Reynolds/Annex Room 106," she shook her head and cried, "You poor thing!"

"Why?"

"Well, everybody says he thinks he's teaching high school, or college. Why he wants to teach seventh graders ...," she shook her head again, "well, it beats me!"

This only made me more anxious to meet him. On that first day of school, I climbed the stairs from the basement up to the first floor and Room 106. It was a large room with a twenty-foot ceiling, with six fluorescent lights suspended ten feet down. A dull, old maple paneling covered the side wall, there were large blackboards at both ends of the room, and on the west side of the room rose a line of enormous windows, fifteen feet high, nearly reaching the top of that wall.

He sat at his desk in the corner, staring at us as we entered, not even acknowledging our arrival; his stare made me turn my eyes away, almost apologetically, and I glanced around for a seat. I took one in the third row, near the middle of the classroom. Once seated I looked again. He kept his eyes on the door, studying each new arrival. He had a big jaw, a large nose, and a flat-top haircut — mostly black hair, but with lots of gray around the ears, too. He had a weathered face, strong and well-lined. I would have guessed that he was at least ten years older than my father, although I soon learned that he was just 40. He wore a brown tie, and an old brown sport coat which sagged around his shoulders.

The bell rang. Two more students came in and found a seat. He stood up. He wasn't tall, not quite six feet, but inside that jacket, which still appeared to be one or two sizes too large, there was a hard, muscular chest.

"Good morning."

I joined a few others in answering, "Morning."

He nodded.

"Welcome to your Social Studies class. My name is Mr. Reynolds." He took attendance, showing no difficulty with any of the names. "Please stay in those seats you are in," he said, "unless I find it necessary to move you." We exchanged glances. Many of us sat up.

"A couple of words about myself," he continued. "This is my second year at Riverdale. Graduated from the University of Michigan, in the officer's training corps for the Navy; flew with the Navy, then joined the Air Force when we became a branch of the military in '47. Am still a member of the Air Force Reserves, over in New York." He stepped out from behind his desk, which sat at a diagonal there in the right hand corner of the room. His pants were baggy, too.

"Have chosen to teach history for two or three years while I get a master's degree, then hope to teach college. Coach football and baseball, so guys, hope to see some of you there. Tryouts begin Friday, by the way. My wife and I have three children, we're expecting a fourth. We live in Stamford."

He stood with his hands behind his back, not moving. I was reminded of commanding officers, in the war movies I had seen, as they addressed their troops.

"As far as my goals and expectations here, I require thirty minutes of homework almost every night. Don't do the homework, don't expect anything better than a C. You're getting ready for high school now. Expect you to be responsible for material assigned. And expect you to be willing to contribute to class discussions, voluntarily or not."

Again we turned to our classmates, sharing worried looks — and our surprise. Lynn's words had not prepared me for this. Ian was here, two rows over to my left. His mouth was half-open: there was disbelief, and distress, in his eyes, in the scowl gathering on his face. There were five or six other familiar faces from West School. Cindy was here, as well, sitting two seats in front of Ian, in the far left corner of the room, up in the first row. I could see that she was nervously tapping her desk with both hands, her head down the whole time — as if trying, I thought, to shut some of this out.

"Material to be covered," Mr. Reynolds continued, turning to the board and picking up a piece of chalk. He began to write — an odd print, I thought, all capitals, at various angles. "They come under these four headings."

After pounding the chalk into the board as if he were angry, these four categories appeared:

        CURRENT EVENTS
        HISTORY
        GOVERNMENT
        GEOGRAPHY

He was back in front of the first row.

"I begin with the assumption that you know almost nothing, next to nothing about the important issues of today." This seemed unfair, I thought, remembering Mrs. Schwartz, and our projects for her. "Who here can tell me what Khrushchev is doing in Laos, or in Berlin, with the help of the East Germans, or in Cuba, with the help of Castro?" I almost raised my hand, and then decided not to. "These are fundamental problems today. My years in junior and senior high school taught me almost nothing about the facts of the world as it is today. The Air Force was my education. I feel obligated to teach you some of what I have learned."

I looked around again. Ian's scowl had almost become a sneer; he pulled down on his bangs, as if to cover his eyes. Then he flipped his notebook open and took out a pen, noisily, as if disgusted with all that he was hearing. Cindy, though, appeared fascinated; she was looking up now, studying Mr. Reynolds intensely. She was still tapping on her desk, but more softly than before.

"Current events!" Mr. Reynolds exclaimed, and he went back to the board and attacked it with these headings:

> AFRICA (ALGIERS, CONGO)
> BERLIN
> INDOCHINA (LAOS, CAMBODIA, VIETNAM)
> LATIN AMERICA (CUBA)
> UNITED NATIONS (NUCLEAR TEST BAN)

"Five key areas we will try to learn something about this year." He put down his piece of chalk and grabbed the newspaper on his desk, unfolded it, and held it up.

"As a way to get started, as a way to touch on many events, will read you headlines of *The New York Times* in the morning." He waved the paper above his shoulders, much as Mr. Saarinen had lifted his Bible in our Sunday School class, I recalled, before finding his passage, with his standard introduction, "... as we read in the word of God," or "as it says in the Holy Scriptures."

"The headlines," Mr. Reynolds went on, "can give you some feeling for the news with which you should become more and more familiar. As you will see, many of the problems that the United States and the President must confront concern these five areas up here on the board."

Several times his eyes shifted over to my left as he spoke. He crossed the front of the room, towards Cindy's desk, and then headed down the aisle between that row of chairs and the wall.

"Listen to this morning's headline." He was nearing Ian's desk. Ian seemed engrossed in drawing something on the inside cover of his new notebook; his pen was making large strokes. Mr. Reynolds stopped beside his desk.

"Gibson, is it?"

"Gilbert," Ian replied, without looking up, not appearing at all ruffled.

"Listen to this morning's headline, Gilbert." Mr. Reynolds was annoyed. It all seemed quite familiar to me: Ian acting as if he didn't care, exasperating a new teacher. I didn't understand it, but I wasn't worried. It never lasted. By the end of sixth grade we all knew how much Mrs. Schwartz liked Ian, no matter how many times she caught him off in his own world, daydreaming, or lost in a book — inevitably any book except the one we were working on in class.

Ian put his pen down, with great nonchalance, and gazed straight ahead.

"Who knows, you might learn something," Mr. Reynolds added, as he brought the *Times* back up to his face and read:

Kennedy Pledges Any Steps to Bar Cuban Aggression/ Says U.S. Would Protect Hemisphere From Threat Posed by Soviet Arms/ President Sees No Evidence of 'Significant' Increase in Castro's Military Power

He continued his walk outside that first row. "All this," Mr. Reynolds said, "from a statement the President offered on Cuba yesterday. That's one critical issue he will have to deal with, whether he likes it or not."

His eyes looked back to the front page of the *Times*. "Let's see what else," he said, coming forward now between the first and second rows. "One of our spy planes flew over Russia. The Kremlin is making the usual threats:

Soviet Protests U-2 Flight Over Sakhalin Off Siberia/ Moscow Reiterates 1960 Threat to Retaliate at Bases Used by U.S.

What else?", and soon he had read three other headlines — an East German "slain" in Berlin, the civil war in Algeria possibly ending, two Negro children trying to enter an all white school in the south — and he was standing in front of the class again.

"Much of this might not make sense today, but I want you to have at least a vague idea of what is happening in the world. As the year goes along," he said, looking confident, but still without a smile, "you'll come to understand many of the major events taking place in our world. Often it is not very nice news. But these are the facts. You have a nice, quiet little town here in Riverdale — 'The Next Station to Heaven,' you call it, right? Am convinced that it won't hurt you a bit if you and your nice little fairy tale world here are forced to listen to a little more truth once in a while, even if just for five minutes first period every day. OK?"

I leaned forward and caught Ian's eye, and he responded by shaking his head, as if to say, "Can you believe this guy!", and then, briefly, staring at Mr. Reynolds and doing his fish imitation — sucking his cheeks in and unrolling his lips, protruding them, and opening and closing the little hole in front, bobbing his head up and down as he did so. I was amused — I almost laughed out loud — but more than anything I was nervous for him. What if Mr. Reynolds noticed?

I could not be disrespectful with adults in this way. Besides, I wasn't upset. He was going to challenge me. I liked that. Whether I liked him or not — and from what

Lynn had told me few students did — that hardly seemed to matter.

Our assignment for the first night was to find at least fifteen countries in Europe and to name which of them were Communist. Mr. Reynolds said he was sure we had an atlas or an encyclopedia at home, and he wanted us to start to learn to use both. He also said we could ask for help from our parents.

That evening I went downstairs to show my father the assignment, while my mother and Lynn finished getting supper ready. It still seemed somewhat odd, to have him home so soon. Of course he had been home when he was sick in February and March, moving stiffly around the house in his blue bathrobe. But this was different. While in New York — except for those two springs when he showed up at the Little League field shortly after 5 p.m. — he usually came through the front door after my brother and sisters and I had finished supper, close to seven o'clock. He and my mother would then eat alone, in the library.

I had a list of twenty countries, but I did not know which were Communist. I explained the assignment to my father. He rested his Winston cigarette on the ash tray beside him, took my notebook, and checked off eight countries. He asked about my classes. He said he looked forward to meeting Mr. Reynolds.

"You've been lucky with some of your teachers, haven't you?"

He was probably thinking of Mrs. Schwartz, but immediately I thought of Mr. Saarinen, and I think he did, too, as he added, "—in school. As long as you are pushed here, it

44

would be nice," he added, "not to have to send you away to school." My parents had mentioned boarding school before, for Lynn and me. "But that's a long time away. Not to worry about for a long time."

My father had gone away to school in eighth grade, my mother in ninth grade. I did think about it sometimes. At tennis camp, up in Vermont, I had been homesick. Still, it had been a confusing year. No one told me much about why my father had gone to Cedar Grove. I tried to ask him, once, before I left for camp. He just said it was over. "I needed the rest and it's behind us, so let's leave it there, OK Tommy?" We had not had the baseball together — not only the season with the Tigers, but the Saturdays and Sundays, too, the many hours spent out on the front lawn, when he would hit me grounders and give me batting practice, and, as he had done so often, since I had turned ten, teach me how to pitch. I had begun to feel less comfortable when we were together. And for some reason I did not seem to be as worried, up in the Green Mountains, during July. I even felt relieved, at times, to be away from home. Some of the older campers talked about their boarding schools. President Kennedy had gone away to school. Maybe it would be a good idea.

My mother called us to dinner.

"Thanks again, Dad," I said, as he got up from his chair.

"Anytime, Tommy." He took a final drag on his cigarette and crushed it in the ash tray and then blew all the smoke out in a quick short breath. He put his left hand around my neck and gave it a gentle squeeze. "This is part of what The Sports Shop should mean. To hardly see you at all for an entire week, it wasn't right. We won't have to wait for Saturday to throw the ball around."

He knew I started football on Friday. On Thursday afternoon, at 5:30, I was outside shooting baskets when his gray VW appeared at the end of the driveway. He beeped at me and I waved back; he turned up the semicircle, disappearing behind the trees and bushes bordering the driveway, and parked in front of the house. I heard him get out of the car and shout, "Catch in five, Tommy?"

"Great!" I answered.

I took a few more shots. Six for ten and Debbie likes me, I told myself. I went three for ten with my twelve-foot jump shot from the corners, and so combined the jump shots with four lay-ups — and got my six for ten the second time. I heard the front door open, and I rolled the basketball towards the garage and began a run across the middle of the front yard. "It's Tommy McDonald," he said. McDonald was the small wide receiver for the Philadelphia Eagles who had become one of my football heroes, largely because of his name, and his size. My father threw a strike from the driveway. Then he jogged my way, and once within fifteen yards he made a cut in the direction of the stone wall. I made a good throw; my hand was just getting big enough to throw a spiral with that old Duke football, my father's since high school. Then I took off, back across the yard and circling down towards the spruce tree. He hit me with a soft pass ten feet in front of the tree. And on it went, for half an hour. It felt great to play catch again.

The junior high school had four seventh grade teams. Mr. Reynolds coached the Lions; I played for the Colts. The other two teams that fall were the Eagles and the Bears. We practiced or played every Monday, Wednesday, and Friday.

On Tuesdays and Thursdays I soon began to walk down from school to work at The Riverdale Sports Shop. My father told me if I wanted to, I could earn a dollar for coming in to help out for an hour-and-a-half or two hours twice a week. "We could really use you," he said. It was fine with me. I helped clean up the packing room, did some sweeping, ran errands, or put the new boxes of sneakers or skates or ski boots in their proper place, back in the storage room. I enjoyed it. Everyone who worked there was nice to me. I didn't get any free footballs or new tennis rackets, but my father did save some of the posters that were yellowing a bit — of Paul Hornung, Jimmy Brown, Rod Laver, and quite a new one of Mickey Mantle — and gave them to me after my second week at the store. At home, Danny and I used up an entire roll of scotch tape as we put up all four posters around the walls of our room. Mickey went over my bed.

I no longer had to hide my hero-worship of Mickey Mantle from my father, as long as I didn't cheer for New York, too. My father hated the Yankees; he still rooted for his Washington Senators, or at least hoped they would not finish in last place, as they were about to do again. But it was my father who had assured me that it was OK to look up to the Yankee center fielder. During the 1961 World Series, when Mickey had played, briefly, against Cincinnati, everyone could see he was playing in pain. He had just had surgery on his hip. When he stepped up to bat in the fourth game of the Series and the camera showed the blood in his right hip coming through the uniform, my father had remarked, "That's something. Pretty damned gutsy." And when Mickey lined a single to deep left center and hobbled down to first — it would have been a double on most days — and a pinch-runner came in for him, I was thrilled. And my father said, "Really something. Gotta hand it to him."

And now with the Yankees having the pennant sewn up, there in late September, I looked forward to seeing a healthy Mickey back in the World Series. Now it was just a question of whether the Giants could catch the Dodgers.

"If at any time the Communist build-up in Cuba were to endanger or interfere with our security in any way ... then this country will do whatever must be done to protect its own security and its allies."

President Kennedy
from his press conference
Sept. 13, 1962

CHAPTER FIVE

Thy Kingdom Come

I RESPECTED MR. REYNOLDS. That first month, I felt I was learning a lot from him. It did bother me that he was so critical of President Kennedy at times. I realized Uncle David might have made similar remarks. "The Harvard-Yale rivalry lives on," my mother once said, when I asked her about my uncle's unkind words about the President. But my uncle still worked for the President, as it seemed to me he was doing. And he was never as harsh as Mr. Reynolds could be.

Harsh, and sarcastic, and once or twice quite emotional. On September 13 he encouraged us to view the President's press conference that evening at 6 p.m. Lynn and I joined my parents to watch for a while, though neither of us stayed. The next morning Mr. Reynolds read the headline to us:

Kennedy Hits At War Talk;
Sees No Cuba Threat Now,
Says U.S. Would Crush One

"The President says here, let me see," and he searched for the passage, "he says he hopes that 'the future record would show that the only people talking about a war and invasion at this time are the Communist spokesmen in Moscow and Havana, and that the American people, defending as we do so much of the free world, will in this nuclear age, as they have in the past, keep both their nerve and their head.'" Mr. Reynolds almost threw the paper on his desk as he commented, "I don't know what 'the nuclear age' has to do with it." He looked away. I followed his eyes: the two maple trees outside the big windows there on our right were so full of leaves they blocked the view to South Street. Mr. Reynolds seemed to be talking to himself, thinking out loud, as he continued: "Can't you be a good American and talk about war anymore? God, it's as if he's forgotten what he fought for as a Navy man in World War II!"

Mr. Reynolds was the only teacher I had ever known who would occasionally slip in a swear word like this. And he never apologized about it.

Later in the month he ordered copies of *Time* magazine for each of us, the current issue with James Monroe on the cover, and we learned about the Monroe Doctrine. It interested me to see that a policy of the fifth President was still President Kennedy's policy as well. "At least the President *claims* it is the policy of our government," Mr. Reynolds told us, rather skeptically. "Whether he'll really follow through remains to be seen."

During the same week Mr. Reynolds informed us that as a member of the Air Force Reserves, he could still be called up in case of a national emergency.

Debbie Myers was in my Sunday School class. This was the best part about going to church that fall. She often wore her dirty-blond hair in pigtails at school, but in church she always let it fall down to her neck. She was very popular. At the Junior High, in the elections on September 25, we voted her Student Council Secretary. I was flattered when she told me I should have run for Treasurer.

I liked the book we were asked to read, *Men and Women of the Old Testament*; but classes were nothing like Mr. Saarinen's. I knew that Debbie was pleased. The year before, when Mr. Saarinen had started to talk about being reborn and being ready for Christ's return, she had stopped coming downstairs. Our classes were held in the basement, one huge space, with "classrooms" curtained off from each other. Throughout the spring Debbie had stayed in the church hall with the adults, while the rest of us filed out, on cue, as soon as our parents began to sing the second verse of the second hymn.

But Debbie loved our new Sunday School teacher, Mrs. Wilson, so now she was always there. We read about Adam and Eve for the first Sunday, Cain and Abel the second, and Noah for the third class, the last weekend in September. The eight-page story of the flood and the rainbow and the survival of Noah's family made me anxious to read the Bible's version. I had not picked up the Bible since Mr. Saarinen's class had ended. I read Genesis 6-9 in my room that week, after Danny had gone to sleep. It reminded me of Christ coming again, to judge, to punish the wicked. I loved the image of the rainbow. I had seen several in Sandy Harbor across the bay at the end of a storm. They added a nice ending to the story. And yet I reread the passages that reminded me of how angry God could be, of how he had chosen to destroy everyone, except for Noah and his family. "I have determined to make an end of all flesh; ... behold I will destroy them with the earth." "I will bring a flood of waters upon the earth, to destroy all flesh in which is the breath of life from under heaven; everything that is on the earth shall die."

My prayers at night often ended with the Lord's Prayer. One phrase troubled me, especially as it came so early in the prayer: "Thy kingdom come." I did not want Christ to come, not now, at age twelve. I did not want to see Him in the sky, beginning the Day of Judgment, as Mr. Saarinen had described it. It made it hard to say those words, and I tried to hurry by them, tried not to think about them. When I had started to read the Gospels of John and Matthew the year before, and when my father had gone away in April, I liked to think of Jesus' words to the disciples, in that boat, in the middle of the storm: "Do not be afraid." And of those brave words in Psalm 23: "Yea, though I walk through the valley of the shadow of death, I will fear no evil...." I thought of myself as being afraid of too many things. Reading about Noah that week, I was reminded of my fear.

Mrs. Wilson, gray and grandmotherly, never spoke to us about Judgment Day. That Sunday, discussing Noah, I asked her if the Second Coming wasn't another time when God would be very angry, and make the wicked suffer very much. She seemed a bit surprised, and said, "No, Tommy, God is very forgiving." I glanced at Debbie. She frowned at me.

October 1

The pennant race between the Dodgers and the Giants finished in a tie, and on October 1 they began their two-out-of-three game playoff. I learned this from looking at the *Times* on Monday morning. That day, and for much of the next two weeks, the playoffs and the World Series were front page news, so I usually had a look at some of the headlines Mr. Reynolds would read us. The *Times* had its most dramatic headline that morning — three huge lines, all the way across the top of the page — about the black student, James Meredith, trying to enter the University of Mississippi, with federal troops there to enforce desegregation. The sports pages had a picture of Mickey hitting his 30th home run in the final game of the regular season. He had gone two for three, and finished second to Pete Runnels for the batting title, .326 to .321. In spite of missing nearly a quarter of the season, he was said to have a good chance of being named the American League's Most Valuable Player again. I hoped so.

In Social Studies class that morning Mr. Reynolds showed us that huge headline on page one and told us, simply, "This has to do with some events in Mississippi. And integration." It was another headline,

*Khrushchev Invites Kennedy to Moscow,
White House Studies Bid for Berlin Talk*

that he read and commented on for five minutes, discussing how "useless, or possibly dangerous" it would be right now if Kennedy went to see Khrushchev, and how the last summit conference had been such a failure. Once home that afternoon, after football practice, I found the *Times* and went upstairs to watch the end of that first playoff game — Willie Mays had two home runs, and the Giants won — and read those three lines marching across the top of the page once again. I studied the series of pictures: of the Governor of Mississippi speaking, looking angry; of U.S. troops at the state university, and James Meredith; and of men and women bleeding. I wondered why Mr. Reynolds never spoke about any of this.

I also cut out the two front-page articles on Berlin to help me with the paper I was working on for Social Studies, due in two weeks. Many stories about Mr. Reynolds' war record passed around the school. According to one story he had been among the first to fly into Berlin during the 1948 airlift.

October 3-5

Wally Schirra's Sigma 7 took off from Cape Canaveral at 8:14 Wednesday morning. We watched the liftoff in Mrs. Brady's homeroom class, before school, and listened to Walter Cronkite describe how the first orbit was going. This time Cindy did not cry. She did not even seem upset.

Upstairs, though, once first-period class had started in Room 106, Mr. Reynolds was quick to point out how far behind we were in the space race.

"The fact is that while we pride ourselves on our scientific know-how, ever since Sputnik we've just been trying to catch up. Schirra is supposed to circle the globe until supper time. Well, Nikovich and Popovich, whatever their names are, both went up in August for — what was it? — three or four days! We ought to stop fooling ourselves."

The Giants beat the Dodgers 6-4 that afternoon, and the next day, when I walked down to the store after school, I was surprised to see a TV on a counter near the shoe department. The World Series was just getting under way out in San Francisco. Many customers, as well as employees, stood around to watch an inning or two before moving on. Whitey Ford out-pitched Billy O'Dell, and the Yankees won, 6-2.

On Friday morning I read the front-page article about the game, and glanced at the other headlines. In first period Mr. Reynolds read a few lines from one of those front-page stories, and then startled me when he slammed the paper down on his desk.

"It's insulting," he said. "I'll tell you one thing—," he went on, pressing his hand from his temple back over his flat top, slowly, and then putting both hands into the back pockets of his baggy khaki pants; "—I'll tell you, if the government could make up its mind and save Cuba through an invasion, the real thing, no Bay of Pigs, then I would be damn glad to go. Damn glad. I could be called up anyway, but for Cuba, for our national security, to stop Khrushchev from knocking on our front door, hell, I'd go."

"I think he's a little cracked," Ian said to me, as we headed out of the Annex for the Math class that we also took together, over on the top floor of the Main Building.

"What do you mean?"

"I mean he's nutso! Psycho!"

"Come on, Ian, he's not that bad."

"You don't think so? Really? God, Tommy, listen to him! It's obvious he lost a few marbles fighting a few too many missions over Korea. It's like he's still in the pilot seat, you know, as if he's still fighting the Commies over there. He doesn't even know the war is over!" We were outside now, in the parking lot — the long way between the two buildings — but avoiding the crowd of students on the main walkway, where they were so packed together they could hardly move. With a book in each hand, Ian raised both arms out, arranged his hands to look like guns — thumbs up, index fingers pointed at his target — and directed a volley of bullets at the Main Building: "Ba-da-da-da-da-da-da-da-da!"

"What are you doing?" I asked, a little embarrassed, but amused, too, as Ian lifted his imaginary artillery at the second floor, and then the third floor.

"Killing Commies of course," he cried. "Ba-da-da-da-da-da-da!" His bullet-like noises were growing louder.

"Losing your marbles, Gilbert?" Jerry called out from the walkway.

"Not me!" Ian yelled, smiling, but riled up, too, now spraying his bullets in their direction. "It's Lieutenant Reynolds, U.S. Air Force, ba-da-da-da-da-da-da-da-da-da! At your service, over Korea! Ba-da-da-da-da-da-da-da-da-da-da! Soon over Berlin! Ba-da-da-da-da-da-da-da-da! Cuba! Ba-da-da-da-da-da-da-da! Anywhere you want to send me!" And he finished with a loud explosion, "KABOOM!" and let his arms drop, and laughed.

"Go get 'em Lieutenant!" several guys responded, enjoying Ian's outburst. I doubted if they knew how furious he was. Others who looked our way seemed puzzled by Ian's hysterics. I was glad he was through. He was quiet the rest of the way to Math class. When I glanced over I saw that he spent much of the period looking out the window.

Behind his back, Ian began to call Mr. Reynolds "Soldier Boy," after the song popular earlier that year, by The Shirelles. But I did not join in. I did not want to make fun of someone I respected. I was sure Mr. Reynolds meant well. He was pretty unusual, but I hardly thought he was "cracked." I had no reason, that first week of October, to be angry with him.

Thy Kingdom Come   57

"... and Abraham went and took the ram, and offered it up as a burnt offering instead of his son."

Genesis 22:13

CHAPTER SIX

Isaac

HURRICANE CELIA HAD NOT REACHED US back in mid-September, and when Hurricane Daisy passed by Long Island Sound that first weekend of October, it only brought more rain and some strong winds to Riverdale. As we drove to church that Sunday morning, I saw few signs of damage. The full trees on either side of Bayberry Hill still reached across to each other, forming a kind of roof over our heads. The leaves were just beginning to turn. Many branches, though, were down. Twice, where branches blocked the road, my father stopped the car and jumped out to drag them off to the side. My parents told us that Padanaram Harbor and Boston might get hit badly, and then they began to talk of what had happened back in 1955, in Sandy Harbor, with Hurricane Diane. They spoke of the rocks that came within forty feet of our house, and of the many summer houses torn off their foundations, floating miles away.

"Do you remember any of that Lynn, Tommy?" my father asked. "Yes," we answered together. They reminded us that we had stayed up at Nana's house for two days, and that many other people, too, had come to her house for safety. I recalled the 1957 hurricane even better, when we again retreated to Nana's. I had looked down at the bay through binoculars from her second floor, with the windows rattling in front of me, and had been alarmed to see that row of trees down to our house twisting and twirling, like spinnakers flapping out of control; and beyond them, even more amazing, to see the way the water pounded into the sea wall and sent spray forty or fifty feet into the air. Whenever I saw *The Wizard of Oz* on TV, and watched as Dorothy and Toto tried to hurry home to safety before the tornado hit, it was those hurricanes I thought of, there in Sandy Harbor, and those days when we stayed at Nana's and looked out at the fierce winds and the rough sea.

"You've been lucky, really," my father told us. "You still haven't seen just how dangerous a hurricane can be."

Although he mentioned neither James Meredith nor Mississippi in his Children's Sermon, I knew what Reverend Marshall was referring to as he declared that "God would be mad if a Negro man could not go to school with others just because of the color of his skin." Then the minister surprised me with a prayer "for the families of those who have been killed by Hurricane Daisy." I thought of Jesus, and how He had calmed those seas, and had told His disciples, "Do not be afraid." I wondered why He would not save the lives of these men and women. Why He would not interfere.

This only added to my confusion as I went to Sunday School class, thinking of my questions about the Abraham and Isaac story we had been assigned that week. It again had caused me to open my Bible. But the Bible's version puzzled me even more. The story in my Sunday School book described Abraham's pain, and Isaac's confusion, but Genesis told the story in an amazingly matter-of-fact way.

> When they came to the place of which God had told him, Abraham built an altar there, and laid the wood in order, and bound Isaac his son, and laid him on the altar, upon the wood. Then Abraham put forth his hand, and took the knife to slay his son.

I read it twice. There were many references to a "burnt offering"; I went to the dictionary to look it up. Maybe it meant something different, I thought, than what it implies; maybe it didn't really mean they would burn him. But there it was, right after "burnt":

> **burnt offering** — An offering, such as a slaughtered animal, burned on an altar as a religious sacrifice.

There were so many questions I had. So much I wanted to ask about Isaac's silence, what Abraham could be thinking, why God would do this. But my questions had little to do with what Mrs. Wilson wanted to review that Sunday morning, the first fifteen minutes of class. Mrs. Wilson, who told us she had taught high school English when she was young, liked to discuss characters, conflict, and theme. The theme that morning, she explained, was Abraham's faith. And then she finally turned to "the character of Isaac." "This young boy," she told us, "obeys, does what is asked, does not scream or rebel; both show this capacity for faith, a faith God rewards with this miracle, the appearance of the ram." This, I was sure, did not represent how Isaac felt. Debbie didn't think so either.

"I feel really sorry for him," she said. "It doesn't seem fair."

"It's especially not fair to Abraham and Sarah," Mrs. Wilson responded, "who were afraid they would never have a child. That's why it is such an enormous test of his faith." Then she and Debbie, and a few others, spent much of the rest of class on that first part of the story, and the promises to Abraham about his descendants, and a son, and the doubts he and Sarah had to conquer.

I felt angry, and remained silent.

When my mother asked me what was wrong on the way home from church, I answered, "Nothing."

After lunch my father asked me outside for a game of catch. He threw harder to me this year. I had caught four touchdowns for the Colts in our Friday games, but was beginning to feel that catching passes and running back kicks was all I could do well. My father left work early to see a couple of those games, and afterwards had given me advice on how to improve my blocking and tackling. "Don't hit so high," he said, after one game. "With your size — I had the

Isaac 61

same problem — we've got to hit low." But I did not seem to be making much progress. At least I could catch the ball. As I held on to his bullets that Sunday, I loved it when he smiled and roared, "Great catch." After twenty minutes he called Danny and Beth out, and we had a game of touch football. Then we all went inside to watch the third game of the World Series, the first home game for the Yankees.

My "seat" in my parents' bedroom was on the floor in front of my father's bed, leaning back against his footboard. I sat there rooted to my spot and pulled for Mickey to do well, silently, while still hoping that Willie Mays and the Giants could win the Series. Mickey singled in the seventh that Sunday afternoon when the Yankees scored their three runs, and though Willie Mays doubled to lead off the ninth, and Ed Bailey homered to make it 3-2, the rally ended there.

I found it easier, that fall, to be against New York. New York was connected somehow to my father's illness. The city had hurt him. It was easier now, not to cheer for the Yankees.

So I was glad when the Giants evened the series at 2-2 the next day, on Chuck Hiller's grand slam in the seventh. But Ralph Terry beat Jack Sanford on Wednesday, 5-3, and the series returned to the West Coast.

※

I continued to go to my father's store most every Tuesday and Thursday. My favorite time was walking through the store with my father when we left at 5:30. As we took our walk he offered a comment or two for everyone, and sometimes stopped to ask a question about how the day had been, or about an item, "When will these skis start to move?"

"Who do we sell these rifles to?" "Does the Winter Club sell any of this same hockey equipment?" Some evenings, though, he just joked around with the salesmen, and his loud laugh rang through the store. Everyone called him "Mr. Chapman," everyone except the vice-president, Mr. Thompson, whose bald head reminded me of President Eisenhower. The way my father seemed so much in charge, the way his voice boomed across the store, it reminded me of those many springs when he had been my coach.

Sometimes, as we drove home, I felt he spoke to me as the President of the company, and not so much as my father. He quizzed me about employees, how they treated customers, how helpful they seemed, how hard they worked. That Thursday, though, he asked me about my classes, and Mr. Reynolds.

"We're going to a PTA meeting at your school next week. I look forward to meeting him. What are you working on now?"

I listed a number of the topics we had been studying. When I told him we were doing projects on current events, and that mine was Berlin, he was quick to say, "How would you like to get in a few words from Washington?"

"You mean Uncle David?"

"Exactly. Sure, he'd love it."

As soon as we were home my father led me in to the library and called the State Department. "He's often there until seven o'clock," my father said, after dialing the number, and soon Uncle David was on the line, and my father was off to get me a pen and a pad of paper, and I talked with "Washington," and took many notes, for half an hour.

Isaac

October 15

My parents went to the Parents and Teachers Association open house on Monday. Our reports for Mr. Reynolds had been due that morning, and he told us he would leave our projects out for our parents to see. Then we were to read and discuss our reports in class over the next two weeks, so that by the end of the following week, U.N. Week, October 22 — 26, we would, as he put it, "have a better idea of some of the conflicts that world body, and our world leaders, must tackle here in 1962."

Mrs. O'Brien, the baby sitter, let us watch more TV than my parents would have allowed. We saw "To Tell the Truth" together. Then Mrs. O'Brien put Danny to bed. The rest of us stayed up to watch "I've Got a Secret." At 8:30 I went to my room to start *The Yearling*, my outside reading for English — due in November. Danny was asleep, so I could turn on my light on the double lamp between our beds. Around 9 p.m. I heard the car come in the driveway. Soon after, my mother gave my door a gentle knock. "We're home," she whispered. "You awake?"

"Hi Mom."

She peeked in and gave a look at Danny, in the bed closest to the door, and laughed softly: his left thumb was in his half-open mouth, and his index finger was in his nostril, and he mumbled something in his sleep that neither of us could understand. I laughed, too. "Come on in," she said. I closed my book and crept around Danny's bed and went into their bedroom. Lynn was already there. We quizzed our parents about who they had seen and what our teachers had said about us.

They had gone to all of Lynn's classes and most of mine; they did not get to meet Mr. Knapp, my Science teacher.

"All your teachers seem very nice," my mother said.

"'Nice' might not be the right word for Reynolds," my father added, from behind the bathroom door.

"No, he wasn't terribly friendly, was he? Very intense." My mother was about to enter the bathroom, but she looked at me and asked, "But you *do* like his class, don't you?"

I nodded.

My father came out of the bathroom. They kept doing this for the next few minutes, taking turns going in and out.

"Not one to suffer fools gladly, that's for sure," my father said, passing my mother. "Still, I liked the Lieutenant. Quite a bit. Not a lot of laughs in class, true Tommy?"

"Yes."

"He certainly seems dedicated," my mother said, returning, taking the two barrettes out of her hair, and putting them on her bureau. "Though I'm not sure *I* could sit in his classroom for forty minutes a day. I'm glad you like him, Tommy, that's the main thing. I'm sure you're learning a lot."

"Did you read my paper?" I asked.

"Oh I'm sorry, of course," my mother said. "Very nicely done."

"Terrific report, son," my father said. "Hope David wasn't giving away any secrets there on what we'd do if they shut down Berlin again. If you get it back this weekend I'm sure he'd love to see it." It was a reminder that my aunt and uncle were coming up to see the Yale-Cornell football game that Saturday in New Haven. "Maybe he'll bring it in to

Isaac 65

JFK," my father added, rubbing the top of my head briefly, and smiling, "and try to set him straight."

My mother sat down on her bed and began to brush Lynn's hair — with my sister turning, as my mother brushed one side, and the back, and then the other side. It was the first time my mother's brown hair, falling to her shoulders, seemed lighter than Lynn's. I knew why; every time my mother came home from the hairdresser that fall her hair seemed to have a few more blond streaks. She and my father both told my sister about her Algebra teacher's concerns. Then my mother asked me how Cindy Mellum was doing. My father closed the bathroom door behind him.

"Good, I guess."

My mother continued brushing Lynn's hair.

"Does she have more friends this year?"

"No, I don't think so."

"Is she any more ... relaxed?"

"I don't know. Sometimes, I guess. Not very."

"She wrote an unbelievable paper." My father stepped out, in his pajamas and his blue bathrobe. "Did you see that, Andy?"

"No, I didn't. The Lieutenant and I talked coaching and football. He has a few old Tigers on his team."

"It was marvelous," my mother said. "About the test ban treaty and U Thant. About nuclear fallout. About Hiroshima. She read Hersey's book and some recent articles; I was just amazed. And it was so sensitive. She's a couple of years ahead of her classmates, in some ways at least. Truly gifted."

I was not totally surprised. I reminded my mother that few of us knew this side of Cindy.

"She hardly ever speaks in class," I said. I was hoping my mother was not going to talk to me again about trying to be kind to Cindy. Fortunately, my father changed the subject.

"So, why haven't you told me about your homeroom teacher?" He was grinning, and Lynn said, "Daddy!" and my mother began to laugh. "Looks to me," he added, "that you were trying to keep Mrs. Brady a secret, is that it?"

My father clenched a fist, and pretended to be upset with me, and I laughed.

My mother had Lynn stand and face her. "You look beautiful, dear," she said, and gave her a goodnight kiss. Lynn started for the door. Then my mother turned to me. "She thinks you're the sweetest boy."

"Tommy, if my French teacher had been that gorgeous I might remember a little more than voulez-vous—"

"Shush!" my mother said, laughing, getting up and putting her hands over his mouth.

I started to head back to my room, too.

"Anyway, Tommy," my father said, "any time you want me to take your homeroom class for you, I volunteer!"

I turned around and smiled.

"Night Dad, night Mom," I said.

"Night boy."

"Night Tommy."

I crept back into my room — Danny tossed a little as the floor creaked under me — and I read a few more pages of my book. I liked it. It was such a foreign world to me. Alone in the woods, tracking a deer, planning to hunt for the bear, Old Slewfoot, with his "Pa".... Then I turned out the light and rolled over to say my prayers.

"On Tuesday morning, October 16, 1962, shortly after nine o'clock, President Kennedy called and asked me to come to the White House. He said only that we were facing great trouble. Shortly afterward, in his office, he told me that a U-2 had just finished a photographic mission and that the intelligence community had become convinced that Russia was placing missiles and atomic weapons in Cuba.

"That was the beginning of the Cuban missile crisis — a confrontation between the two giant atomic nations, the U.S. and the U.S.S.R., which brought the world to the abyss of nuclear destruction and the end of mankind."

Robert Kennedy
from the opening of Thirteen Days

CHAPTER SEVEN

The Fate of Nations

I WATCHED THE SEVENTH GAME of the World Series on Tuesday afternoon at the store. My father told me not to worry about working, just to relax and enjoy it. It was the third and very best matchup between Ralph Terry and Jack Sanford.

Mickey was having a terrible series — two hits in twenty-two at bats, batting .091, as the paper had told me that morning. The sports page had a photograph of Mickey on his right knee, still in the batter's box, slamming his bat down on the ground after popping up during Monday's loss.

He didn't even run it out. My father would not have approved. I had often read of Mickey's terrible temper — of the water coolers he had smashed, the bats he had broken, and the helmets he had kicked around after striking out, or after failing in the clutch. I felt sorry for Number Seven; I hoped he could do well in this last game. I studied him as he stepped into the batter's box. The close-ups showed his fingers moving more restlessly than usual as he gripped the bat. I could see the muscles in his thick neck straining. With the Yankees up just 1-0 in the top of the eighth, and two men on, he ripped a single to right — too hard, though, to bring in Bobby Richardson from second. O'Dell relieved Sanford and got the final out.

My father emerged from his office and joined us. It was nearly 5:15, and business had pretty much come to a stop, but there were over a dozen men and a few women around the TV, salesmen, secretaries, and customers. The Yankee pitcher had only given up two hits the entire game, one a triple by Willie McCovey, a shot to deep center over Mickey's head. Matty Alou led off the bottom of the ninth with a bunt single, but Terry struck out the next two batters, and Alou remained at first. Willie Mays stepped in. My father, beside me, whispered, "Bring him home, Willie." He almost did: he doubled down the right field line, but Roger Maris cut the ball off and gunned it back to the infield to save the run. The Yankee fans around us roared their approval — "How to go, Roger!" — and their relief. My father shook his head and muttered, "Hell of a play." It was fun being around all these men and women; it was almost like being at the game itself. They cheered and protested and shouted as they never would in a normal day at the store. And yet when Terry entered his wind-up, I was amazed at the sudden hush.

The Fate of Nations 69

Willie McCovey stepped up to the plate.

"Don't pitch to him, Ralph!" I heard several plead.

"I've got $5 on this," one man said, "don't let him swing the bat!" They screamed when McCovey sent the first pitch deep to right; my father, far more quietly, urged the ball to "Go fair! Go fair!" — but it curved foul, deep in the right field stands. The Yankee fans again seemed to catch their breath, and to plead for mercy. "Don't do it! Houk, let him walk!" Again a sudden silence. The next pitch came in, McCovey unwrapped that big swing — a bullet, "A shot!" the announcer cried, a line drive on its way to — the second baseman, "Richardson has it! The Yanks win it!" And the men around me celebrated, slapping each other on the back, shaking hands, acting as if — as if they had something to do with it, congratulating each other with, "Hey, great game!" or "Way to go!" On TV the Yankee players came in to hug each other, the infield and the bench pouring in to circle Ralph Terry, and then Mickey and Roger, and finally the pitchers in the bullpen falling all over their teammates, embracing each other, then lifting Terry up on their shoulders. I saw Willie Mays walk into the Giants' dugout, with his head down — not unlike the way my father was walking, I noticed, as he moved away and returned to his office.

October 18

"I'm afraid Uncle David and Aunt Carol won't be able to make it up this weekend." We were driving home from the store, Thursday evening. "Things are quite hectic at the State Department, he tells me. He just called an hour or so ago. Expects he'll have to work all weekend. And this Hurricane Ella may be on its way. Said he hopes he can make the game with Princeton in a few weeks."

I was sorry to hear this. I wanted my uncle to see my paper. I hoped to ask him more questions, and to show him how much I was learning from Mr. Reynolds.

"His work, what he does, it's very important, isn't it, Dad?"

My father looked over at me.

"Yes, it is Tommy." He turned his eyes back to the road. "And he works extremely hard. It can be quite a strain. I wouldn't be surprised if he hardly sleeps at all this weekend. I don't know how he does it. I would go crazy."

I glanced up at him. He was looking in the rear view mirror.

"What?" he asked. There was no snap to it, no judgment, but he expected an answer. "What is it?"

I shook my head. "Nothing."

That evening I read the week's assignment for Sunday School, the chapter on Joseph from our book, *Men and Women of the Old Testament*. Joseph's success and his position as second only to the Pharaoh made me think of my uncle. Both worked for their country's leader, gave him advice, and tried to suggest what might happen next. Looking ahead, predicting events ... I wondered if God still helped people see into the future. No, I thought. We would not be told more than what Christ had given us in the New Testament. As Mr. Saarinen had shown us, the Judgment Day was *what* we knew about our future — we just did not know *when*. If I could be told that there would be seven years

The Fate of Nations

of this, I thought, and seven years of that ... I would then be ... twenty-six. An adult. A man. I liked the end of our story, which spoke of Joseph and Jacob together again after so long, and of Joseph's tears as he embraced his father.

❧

October 20-21

I thought of those tears on Saturday when we drove up the Merritt Parkway to New Haven with four other families and had our picnic and played our game of touch football. Yale won quite easily, 26-8. It was a warm day, so I expected the players would be hot and sweaty when they marched by out of the stadium. But as the Cornell team approached, their cleats scraping and echoing along the road beside us, I looked up at these big men — as they seemed to me — from their white pants and dirtied red jerseys to their faces and their black eye-block, and saw ... more than sweat. Several players were in tears. I had cried over many of my losses in baseball, and after a number of tennis matches. But I had never seen grown men cry before.

Sunday morning, before church, I checked the sports pages of the Sunday *Times* sitting on the kitchen table. I read about the Yale game, and other college games, and the NBA games — their season had just begun, and then about the Giants football game that would be played that afternoon with Detroit. Before going upstairs to change into my Sunday School clothes I took my now customary glance at the front page. There was a big headline about China and India being involved in heavy border fighting. A smaller headline referred to the Pope and the Ecumenical Council meeting that week in Rome. Another one column headline was about Kennedy:

PRESIDENT CUTS HIS TOUR SHORT, FLIES TO CAPITAL

Has Mild Cold — Speculation Rises On Possible Urgent White House Business

There was also a large, dark photograph on the front page. It showed a small village in the foreground and a bright light far away in the distance. The headline read:

U.S. FIRES LONG-DELAYED ATOM BLAST ABOVE PACIFIC

I began to read the article. "A nuclear device the size of the atomic bomb that destroyed Hiroshima in 1945 was detonated above Johnston Island last night. A larger test shot is scheduled for ...."

I felt curious. I knew so little about atomic bombs. Ian had been the only person who had tried to teach me, briefly, when he had done his report the year before. I decided to ask Cindy Mellum the next day if I could borrow one of her books. She had been carrying around a copy of a thin book titled *Hiroshima*. I assumed Hiroshima must have been a little town, if it was once "destroyed" by a bomb.

And then as I got up and folded the front page back I saw the cover of the Sunday *Times* Magazine. It was from an old painting. I looked more closely, and was startled to read the title over the painting: *The Last Judgment.* There was a powerful figure at the center, His arms raised, one above His head, as if preparing to — to do what? — to strike? to hit? The others nearby, to His left, seemed to pull away from Him — and yet all of them, whether amazed or daring or fearful, kept their eyes fixed on Him. It was Jesus. His eyes looked down, as if He did not dare look at all these people, at the mass of figures moving, twisting, reaching out, turning away.... Above the picture there were these words:

Michelangelo's vast masterpiece of the Last Judgment ... gives one much food for thought. We must indeed render an account to God; we and all the heads of state who bear responsibility for the fate of nations.
    Pope John XXIII, during the Ecumenical Council

    I looked back at the painting. This was not quite how Mr. Saarinen had described it for us, in the spring. But again, it seemed as if God was trying to remind me. Had I thought too little about that day? Probably. How soon, I wondered, once again, as I had done so often during the spring, and over the summer, waiting for the next flash of lightning, how soon before Jesus returned? I was lost in these thoughts when my father's sharp words made me jump.

    "Tommy! What are you doing? We're late as it is — hurry up now, get changed! Come on boy, let's go."

    It was drizzling out, and gusty. On the drive over it seemed at times as if it were raining leaves; leaves of all colors took their turns appearing on the windshield, momentarily, before being brushed away. I was told that this bad weather was all we had to show for Hurricane Ella, which had gone out to sea. It was now the fourth hurricane of the season. I wondered if they were part of what Mr. Saarinen would have called "signs."

We walked into church just as the opening verse of the first hymn was being sung:

Come ye thankful people, come
Raise the song of harvest home:
All is safely gathered in,
Ere the winter storms begin.

Church was crowded; there was no row for all six of us. Other latecomers were seated first. My mother led us into two rows — she sat with Beth and Danny, and Lynn and I sat right behind them with my father. Lynn picked up the hymnal and turned to hymn #137, just as the organist started the third verse.

For the Lord our God shall come,
And shall take His harvest home;
From His field shall in that day
All offenses purge away;

Again, the words seemed meant for me. This time it did not sound like a terrible punishment, a frightening judgment. Many people, though, would not be "gathered in," or "harvested"; as Mr. Saarinen had shown me, the Bible was clear about that.

We sang the fourth verse, again asking Christ to return:

Even so, Lord, quickly come
To thy final harvest home;
Gather thou thy people in,
Free from sorrow, free from sin.

I tried not to worry. I tried not to think that Jesus would appear soon. "Do not be afraid." I looked around me. Did Lynn, or my father, or my mother — did Debbie, or anyone I knew, want Judgment Day to come soon? No. Some other time. Long after we were dead. Not now. Not when I was twelve.

"My husband is in those ashes."

from *Hiroshima*, by John Hersey

"... but neither will we shrink from that risk at any time it must be faced."

from President Kennedy's address to the nation
October 22, 1962

CHAPTER EIGHT

Monday, October 22

I WAITED FOR CINDY outside homeroom Monday morning before we climbed the stairs to first period. Her copy of *Hiroshima* was in her arms, on top of her notebook and school books.

"Cindy, I read something about Hiroshima this weekend. Could I borrow your book some time?"

She looked surprised to see me walking beside her, to have me talking with her.

"I don't know. Gee, I have this science report next week and I'm using it, you see, and—," she stopped suddenly to reach inside her blue-rimmed glasses to scratch her left eye. Her rims were even shaped strangely, rising at the top outside corners in a curve, reminding me of pointy little cat ears.

"I'm sorry," I said, "I thought it was about the war with Japan and all and nuclear bombs."

"Oh it is," she said, taking her hand away from her eye and looking straight ahead, "but it's also about burns and radiation." We turned the corner at the landing, by the main door, and climbed the next twelve steps. "Here," she resumed, taking *Hiroshima* from beside her notebook, handing it to me, and — for the first time — looking at me, "take it for a few days. I need it by the weekend, that's all. OK?"

I told her I didn't want to keep her from doing her report, but she insisted I have it.

"Thanks," I said, as we entered Room 106.

"Maybe," she shrugged. I wondered what she meant by this, but she still wouldn't look at me. "It's hard to believe." Her eyes looked sad. "And depressing." She shook her head and turned away to take her seat there in the first row.

It was the longest conversation we had had in nearly a year.

Mr. Reynolds read us only one headline from the *Times* that morning:

>*Capital's Crisis Air Hints
>At Development on Cuba;
>Kennedy TV Talk is Likely*

"A couple of sentences," he went on, "from the article: 'There was an air of crisis in the capital tonight. President

Kennedy and the highest Administration officials have been in almost constant conference all weekend, imparting serious agitation and tension to official Washington.'"

This must be why my uncle had missed Saturday's game. Mr. Reynolds encouraged us to watch the President on TV that night if he did speak. But our teacher did not sound excited about any of these developments.

"It's unlikely anything will happen, however. As a nation we're great at *saying* things as if we mean them, but damned if we *do* anything. Speak boldly at times, yes, but carry a quiet little stick. Afraid of our own strength. We play the mild-mannered gentleman, and do the 'proper thing' — by not acting we show just how weak, and gutless, we really are."

"Gutless." Was he using the word to describe President Kennedy? It seemed so. I could see Mr. Reynolds using this word, or one like it, with his football team. I heard the guys say he was a good coach, a tough coach. My final game had been on Friday; that Monday afternoon the season ended for all of us as Mr. Reynolds' team, the Lions, played the Bears for first place. I wondered if Mr. Reynolds would accuse his own players of being "gutless." I could almost imagine him barking at me, after a missed tackle, "Chapman, dammit, you're *gutless!*" Even if it sometimes seemed true. Not in football, I didn't think. In other ways. More important ways.

I tried to get my mind back on what Mr. Reynolds was saying.

"—has now had six weeks to put together a plan on how to deal with Cuba. You hear the *Times* tell us we might be approaching a crisis. If it's not too late, I suspect that whatever we do will be too mild. Oh, well," and he gave a small shrug, "if he speaks, try to see some of what your President has to say."

"And don't worry," he added, "about the possibility of me disappearing into the service. Am on alert now, I remind you, but again, it's terribly unlikely we'll be called up."

I heard Ian whisper something to the boy in front of him — I could almost hear the words myself — and Mr. Reynolds looked their way.

"Yes, I know you might *like* to see me disappear for a while, Gilbert. Sorry to disappoint you."

Ian glowered, at first, but then he seemed embarrassed. He took his hands away from his mouth and put them on his desk, fidgeting, as if he did not know what to do with them, before finally folding them together. He kept his eyes down for much of the rest of the period.

We listened to Pam and Gary give their reports. Pam spoke about what UNICEF stood for, and what the Children's Fund did; it was a reminder that Halloween was approaching. My plan for that year was to go around the neighborhood with the orange milk carton and trick-or-treat for UNICEF, and then bring in the $3 or $4 I usually collected to be sent to India and Africa. But I would not put on a costume. The year before Lynn came up with the idea of the two of us going out as the Kennedys: I was the President, all dressed up, in my Sunday School clothes, with a bow tie and a top hat; she was Jackie, with her hair puffed up, and lots of eye-shadow and lipstick. It was fun — fun to be greeted by the neighbors, "Oh, Jack and Jackie, what an honor! How nice of you to visit us! Won't you come in!" But I had outgrown costumes now.

Then Gary spoke about the U.N. and the Congo. Gary was Mr. Reynolds' quarterback. In Little League, that spring, he and I had split our two games pitching against each other. He stood there in front of the class and talked to us as easily as if he were having a conversation with friends out in the hallway. I envied him that confidence. I wondered if he ever felt nervous before a big game — such as the playoff with the Bears that afternoon. Probably not.

I often had half an hour after lunch to go play touch football, before going to French class, but that day I walked back into my homeroom — Mrs. Brady was gone, it was her lunch period, too — and read *Hiroshima* instead. After school I stayed to watch the football game. The Lions won easily. Once home I continued to read Hersey's book. My father called us down when supper was ready, and I turned over the corner of page 38, and realized my stomach did not feel well. I placed the book on top of *The Yearling*. I was reading about Mr. Tanimoto's efforts to find his family after the bomb, courageously entering the city while everyone else was trying to escape. As he passed hundreds fleeing the city "every one of them," the book said, "seemed to be hurt in some way. The eyebrows of some were burned off and skin hung from their faces and hands. Others, because of pain, held their arms up as if carrying something in both hands. Some were vomiting as they walked. Many were naked or in shreds of clothing...." As I headed downstairs, I recalled Cindy's warning about this book.

We sat down to eat. I usually loved my mother's lamb, but I wasn't hungry. My father spoke to Lynn and to me, "and you, too, Beth, if you want — I'd like you to watch the President at 7:00, so let's hustle a bit."

"Can't I watch?" Danny said, dropping his fork on his plate, loudly.

My parents tried to explain to him that he wouldn't understand any of it, that he should try to be quiet and play in his room. We rushed through the rest of dinner. My father went upstairs with Danny, and Lynn assured my mother that we could take care of it, so she left, too. Beth and I put the dishes into the dishwasher and cleaned the pots and pans, and Lynn wiped off the stove and the kitchen table and put the leftovers away. I checked the kitchen clock when we were done: 6:56. I hurried upstairs to my parents' bedroom and sat down in front of my father's bed. My mother was already watching the end of the Huntley-Brinkley broadcast. Lynn came in and took her place in the blue armchair near my feet, and Beth followed and lay down on my mother's bed.

My father arrived just as a voice introduced President Kennedy. The TV showed the seal of the President of the United States. Kennedy sat at a desk behind a lectern and two microphones. Behind him were two flags, an American flag on the left, and a dark flag on the right, which I did not recognize.

The bed behind me creaked as my father lay down.

"Good evening, my fellow citizens."

"Turn it up, Tommy, please," my father asked.

I jumped up and increased the volume.

"Thanks."

I sat back down.

"... the purpose of these bases," the President was saying, "can be none other than to provide a nuclear strike capability against the western hemisphere."

The camera was closing in on his face. Now we could only see the very top of the two microphones, and just the gray background. I had noticed before how his eyes seemed rather close together; what I saw now, though, was how tired his eyes appeared. Even his voice sounded restrained, unemotional, that first minute or so. He did not talk in his usual spirited way; there was none of the crisp, cool style I had seen in his press conferences. He glanced down at his speech at the beginning of each sentence, then looked up for five or six words, and then back down again.

"And having now confirmed and completed our evaluation of the evidence and our decision on a course of action," he said, "this government feels obliged to report this new crisis to you in fullest detail."

He told us there were now, or there would soon be — I couldn't tell from the way he said it — in Cuba, "that imprisoned island," he called it, medium-range ballistic missiles "capable of carrying a nuclear warhead for a distance of more than 1,000 nautical miles," and "intermediate-range ballistic missiles capable of striking most of the major cities in the western hemisphere, ranging as far north as Hudson Bay, Canada, and as far south as Lima, Peru."

With all his bending over to read his words, I saw his tongue more than I normally did. And his lower teeth. Not his upper teeth. There would be no broad smiles, no smiles at all, that evening.

He went on. "This urgent transformation of Cuba—," the pronunciation was more like "Cuber" this time, I thought, "—into an important strategic base — by the presence of these large, long-range, and clearly offensive weapons of sudden mass destruction — constitutes an explicit threat to the peace and security of all the Americas."

He quoted several lines from the Soviet government — I liked the way he made it a pattern: "and I quote ... unquote," using their words to show how they had deceived us. His voice grew more assertive, I thought, as he said, "That statement was false." It occurred to me that I should try to say it this way — "quote ... unquote" — when Mr. Reynolds called on me to give my report on Berlin. As in those three or four passages from my uncle: "As David Chapman, assistant to Secretary of State Dean Rusk, says, quote ... unquote." The President quoted Soviet Foreign Minister Gromyko's reassurances to him, commenting that in each case, and here his voice dropped heavily on the last word of the phrase, "That statement was also false."

I was struck by how clean shaven President Kennedy looked, here at 7 p.m. at night. My father's hair wasn't as dark, but by supper time it often seemed as if he needed another shave. What a good, strong chin the President had, I thought. There was toughness in that chin. I thought of Mickey; Mickey had the thicker neck, but the chin, the wide jaw, they seemed to be the same. The President looked angry, in his way, but he was not about to lose control as Mickey might do, when he exploded. Nor would Kennedy swear at the Russians, the way Uncle David might have done, saying something like, "Those damned bastards!" Still, the President was mad.

He continued to look down for his next phrase, but his pace quickened, and the words rolled out more smoothly.

"... and our history, unlike that of the Soviets since the end of World War II, demonstrates that we have no desire to dominate or conquer any other nation or impose our system upon its people. Nevertheless, American citizens have become adjusted to living on the bull's eye of Soviet missiles located inside the U.S.S.R. or in submarines."

Lynn, four feet away in the armchair, had pulled a *Glamour* magazine from off my mother's desk and was looking up and down — at the President, and then at the women, the ads, the articles, and then back up again to Kennedy. His phrases grew choppier. The hard edge to his voice grew sharper.

"But this secret, swift, and extraordinary build-up of Communist missiles ... this sudden, clandestine decision ... is a deliberately provocative and unjustified change in the status quo which cannot be accepted...."

The words were difficult to follow, but they seemed to pound away, as if a hand were silently pounding the desk with each point. I had seen him use his hands so often in his speeches and press conferences — showing conviction and energy, as well as calmness and composure. But in this talk, those hands stayed beneath the lectern, out of sight.

He spoke of the United States being opposed to war, but also being "true to our word." And so action was now necessary. It had already begun, he told us. "And these actions may only be the beginning. We will not prematurely or unnecessarily risk the cost of worldwide nuclear war in which even the fruits of victory would be ashes in our mouth — but," and he looked down once more, at his speech, briefly, before raising his eyes to the camera and declaring, "neither will we shrink from that risk at any time it must be faced."

"Worldwide nuclear war." "Ashes in our mouth." I wanted him to stop. It made me think for a moment of scenes in Cindy's book. Of the city on fire, almost everywhere. Of terrible burns, of people burned so badly they were bleeding to death. Of the incredible numbers I had come across before dinner: 100,000 dead, and another 100,000 wounded. And all from only one bomb. Atomic bombs. They could not only destroy cities, as I was beginning to understand, they could do so much more....

And the phrase — "worldwide nuclear war." Where had I read about this? ... Then I remembered ... wasn't there something about this in his Inaugural Address, something I could not understand the year before when I had given my report for Mrs. Schwartz?

I wasn't sure I could follow the President even now. Winning, he said, would taste like death — "the fruits of victory ... ashes in our mouth" — but if that was the cost, he also seemed to be saying, we would pay it. Maybe I didn't understand. And he was going fast now. I could not keep up.

The several steps already taken, he said, included "a strict quarantine on all offensive military equipment to Cuba...."

"What's that, Dad?" I asked.

"A blockade," he answered. "Like a road block — at sea."

The President was on his second step.

"—Should these offensive military preparations continue, thus increasing the threat to the hemisphere, further action will be justified. I have directed the Armed Forces to prepare for any eventualities...."

I thought of Mr. Reynolds at home in Stamford, watching this, too. I wondered if these steps would please him.

President Kennedy went on to the third step.

"It shall be the policy of this nation to regard any nuclear missile launched from Cuba against any nation in the western hemisphere," he paused, "as an attack," another pause, "by the Soviet Union on the United States, requiring full retaliatory response," and he paused one more time, "upon the Soviet Union. Fourth."

But I did not hear fourth, or fifth, or sixth.

Now it was more clear what he was threatening. The phrase "worldwide nuclear war" made more sense to me now. A "full retaliatory response" was somewhat confusing, and yet the main idea was understandable. My father had taught me the word. "Never retaliate," he had said to me, and to the other pitchers on the Tigers, once, after a game in which two batters were hit, accidentally. "That's not for Little League. Not for kids. Don't you *ever* try to hit another batter."

The President was giving his warning: we *would* pay them back, if they started it. After bombs hit us, lots of bombs would be sent from here to there — to the Soviet Union. It might be the start of World War III. The fighting, the battles, would not be like those I had seen in movies about the Second World War on TV. There would be no submarines seeking the German cruiser, no airplane pilots shooting at each other over the Pacific. Just how it would be different, I would have to find out. I pictured Mr. Tanimoto running by all those people, arms in the air, burned, crying, fleeing from his city....

"Seventh and finally," the President was saying, and I turned my attention back to his words, "I call upon Chairman Khrushchev to halt and eliminate this clandestine, reckless, and provocative threat to world peace and to stable relations between our two nations. I call upon him further to abandon this course of world domination and to join in an historic effort to end the perilous arms race and transform the history of man. He has an opportunity now to move the world back from the abyss of destruction...."

What was an "abyss," I wondered? But I didn't want to interrupt again. "We have no wish to war with the Soviet Union, for we are a peaceful people who desire to live in peace with all other people," he said. At the same time he used the terms "the Soviet threat to peace" and "this latest Soviet threat," and warned that the United States would respond to "any hostile move anywhere in the world ... — including in particular (against) the brave people of West Berlin — ... by whatever action is needed." I wondered what Berlin had to do with this, but I liked the phrase, calling those people brave. Uncle David would have agreed.

He was now saying a few words "to the captive people of Cuba." I could tell he was nearing the end. Lynn was looking at *Glamour* now with even more concentration, apparently reading an article. As the President went on I reached out my foot to the side of her chair to nudge her, and nodded my head toward the TV. She opened her eyes widely, and glared at me; her lips were tight, but I could almost hear her saying: "mind your own business!" Even so, she turned her eyes back to the screen, and watched the final minute.

He was speaking with more concern in his voice. "No one can foresee precisely what course it will take or what costs or casualties will be incurred. Many months of sacrifice and self-discipline lie ahead — months in which both our patience and our will will be tested, months in which many threats and denunciations will keep us aware of our dangers. But the greatest danger of all would be to do nothing."

He spoke with extra forcefulness here. Yes, I was quite sure Mr. Reynolds would be pleased.

"... The cost of freedom is always high," Kennedy said, and he held the word "high" for an additional second or two, "but Americans have always paid it. And one path we shall never choose, and that is the path of surrender," and he paused briefly, before adding, "or submission."

I turned as Beth cuddled close to my mother, her head resting under my mother's chin, her eyes closed. My mother looked worried. She held Beth more tightly.

"Our goal is not the victory of might but the vindication of right," he said, approaching the end of his speech, and the camera began to pull back again, and the microphones and the flags reappeared, "not peace at the expense of freedom, but both peace and freedom, here in this hemisphere and, we hope, around the world. God willing, that goal will be achieved."

He nodded his head, a slight drop to one side, as if — I wasn't sure — it seemed an odd gesture, somehow not quite right.

"Thank you and good night," he said. I studied his face. He did not seem pleased.

Sometimes after the President was on TV my father responded to Kennedy's words with a quick reply — "And goodnight to you, too, Jack" — but not this evening.

"Flip it to 2," my father said, as he lit up a Winston. I did, to Walter Cronkite.

Beth opened her eyes, and started to leave. So did Lynn, taking *Glamour* with her. I did not want to stay either.

"What do you think?" my mother asked.

I thought she was asking me. I did not know how to put it all together. There was something impressive in the bold, dramatic words. They had been serious, angry, and in a small way, hopeful. But more than anything the President had asked me to begin to imagine the possibility of "a worldwide nuclear war," of more bombs like the one that had destroyed Hiroshima ... falling on Moscow, New York, back and forth.

Fallout shelters — for the first time in months I thought about the bomb shelters several neighbors had installed. We would need to hide in one. I imagined that next door the Mills were getting fresh supplies ready, about to take them out to their shelter. Randy would bring lots of Coca-Cola.

And I thought of the President's words, of another possibility — of a victory that tasted like "ashes in our mouth."

"I don't—," I began.

"I wouldn't worry," my father said, more loudly, drowning me out. "Khrushchev's not that crazy. Seems to me that he's giving the Russians a clear line." He took a deep drag on his cigarette, and held the smoke in his chest for five or six seconds before exhaling. "I like it," he added, through the smoke. "I think it's on the money. Firm, strong."

"But frightening, too, isn't it?" my mother added.

Neither of them said a word to Lynn or Beth as they departed. I got up and moved for the door.

"So a Russian ship tries to run through the blockade," my mother was saying, "are they going to blow it up? Is he really willing to start — God knows what — over a few missiles inside of Cuba?"

"Ssshhh," my father demanded, "let's listen." Mr. Cronkite was summarizing the President's main points, and my parents remained quiet as I left the room.

Danny was on the floor, playing on the new hockey set my father had given him the week before for his sixth birthday. He was spinning his players, trying to score with his defensemen from back near his own goal, shooting the marble between the opposing players and his own and on towards the other goal — which had no goalie, I noticed, when I nearly stepped on him, a two-inch masked figure, stick in hand, crouched over, lying there beside Danny's knee.

"Want to play?" he asked.

"No thanks," I said, heading for our bookcase, where I thought I had last seen the *Life* magazine about the President's inauguration.

What was it he had told us, in that speech? I found the special edition buried under a dozen copies of *Sport* and *Sports Illustrated* I had saved over the summer and fall. I turned on my light and sat on my bed and leafed through the photographs for a while before searching for those three passages that had puzzled me so much the previous spring. There they were:

> Man holds in his mortal hands the power to abolish all forms of human poverty — and all forms of human life.
>
> Both sides (must) begin the quest for peace before the dark powers of destruction unleashed by science engulf all humanity in planned or accidental self-destruction.
>
> ... two great and powerful groups of nations ... racing to alter that uncertain balance of terror that stays the hand of mankind's final war.

They were still hard, but I understood these passages better now. The President had been more direct back then. It seemed to me he had been more truthful as well. They were like a prophecy.

Like Joseph, it occurred to me. Predicting the future.

Except that Joseph had figured out how to save lives. How to feed people during the seven years of famine. Seven years of withered corn and thin cows.

The President was saying we as a country would be willing, in spite of the risk and the cost, to "retaliate."

I put his speech back into my drawer. I thought of picking up *The Yearling*, but returned, reluctantly, to "the burned and bleeding" in *Hiroshima*.

It was my father who tapped on my door a little after 9 p.m. to say goodnight. Only my bedside lamp was on; most of the room was dark. He moved around Danny's bed. "Watch out for the hockey set," I whispered, and he said "Thanks," and stepped away from it and came up between our two beds and rubbed my crewcut.

"How are you boy?" he asked.

I tried to speak quietly.

"Fine. You liked the President's speech, Dad?"

He leaned over to look at Danny, and I heard him chuckle a little. He looked back at me and nodded.

"Yes, a good speech, I think. Good and strong. Nothing so belligerent that we — no, I thought it was fine." He began to back away.

"It doesn't worry you?"

He seemed almost amused. He was near the foot of my bed now, and though I couldn't see him well, I imagined a smile on his face.

"Why should it? No. Tommy, boy, remember, I was around your age when Pearl Harbor happened. That was the real thing. That was a war. Here the President is just trying to stop some ships from going to Cuba. It's a little risky, sure, but I'll bet you it doesn't cost a single life."

I knew this voice, full of reassurance. It was the same voice that had told me so many times, after losing a game, and before bed, that I had done well, that we had the next game to look forward to. Those words had often comforted me. They had kept me from harping too much on my mistakes and my disappointment.

But there was no comfort in his words now. How could he *not* be afraid? Was it my fault that I was scared? Was I not being "grown up" enough?

Then he added, more loudly, "Everyone's more careful these days, with these new weapons, so they'll talk it out, save face as best they can — it's what happens now. Besides, Khrushchev isn't totally nuts. He'd have to be suicidal to push this too far." Danny groaned and turned in his sleep. My father circled back around Danny's bed and headed toward the door. "So don't worry, OK?" He was whispering now. "It's going to be fine. Listen," and even in his softer voice I could hear the joke coming, "when it's time to worry, I'll be the first one to run, OK?"

He stood at the door for a moment, waiting.

"Sleep well, boy."

"Night, Dad."

A few minutes later I pulled the covers back and knelt down and prayed.

I prayed for my family. And then, instead of the Lord's Prayer, I said the Twenty-third Psalm. "... Yea, though I walk through the valley of the shadow of death, I will fear no evil: for thou art with me...."

I opened my eyes and looked at my hands in front of me, there in the dark, my hands folded in prayer.... I had the strange sensation of imagining them burned, of seeing the skin melt away, hanging from the bones. I clamped them together, desperately, feeling the skin, folding and refolding them — as if I were playing that childhood game of "Here's the church and here's the steeple." I squeezed them together for one final request. "And God, please help Mr. Kennedy," and I climbed back into bed.

"Since the end of the Second World War, there has been no threat to the vision of peace so profound, no challenge to the world of the Charter so fateful. The hopes of mankind are concentrated in this room...."

> Adlai Stevenson, U.S. Ambassador to the U.N.
> from his speech delivered at the U.N.
> October 23, 1962

"We have won a considerable victory. You and I are still alive."

> Secretary of State Dean Rusk, to his staff
> October 23, 1962

CHAPTER NINE

Tuesday, October 23

THE NEXT MORNING, AND ALL THAT WEEK, many of us were eager to talk about the blockade, and the danger, and the possibilities. When we got on the bus Tuesday a number of eighth graders were in the middle of an argument.

"—and so my father," Bobby was saying, "believes that everyone who stays underground for thirty days will survive. And that we'll bomb Russia to little pieces, just like we did to the Japs."

Ian and I found a seat together, right behind Lynn and her friend, Diana.

Jed, another eighth grader, spoke up. "Sure, maybe we will bomb them to pieces, but what do you think is gonna happen to us? We'll be wiped out, too. There won't be anything left. I think we'll just drive up to my grandfather's, and die together." Many of us stared at him, in disbelief. We wondered what else he had to say, but he was through, as he proved by standing up, rolling down his window, spitting out his gum with authority, "thwop!," and then slumping back into his seat.

"We're going up to our ski lodge in Vermont, if it happens," I heard Diana say, quietly. Lynn turned and we looked at each other for a moment. Maybe she was thinking about Sandy Harbor, too. "It's safer there," Diana added.

Sandy Harbor, up there beside Buzzards Bay, at Nana's, where we had waited out other storms. In her big house, not our little cottage, which could blow away in a hurricane....

Or what about those cabins up in Vermont, near Stowe, at the tennis camp? Yes, that would be much safer, so much farther away from anything. Maybe I could lead my family there, I thought. They wouldn't drop bombs way up north in those mountains, so far from New York City....

Ian, beside me, got up on one knee so that he could be heard in the back. He swept his bangs off his forehead. "The problem is," he began, speaking more slowly than the others, "you'll never make it to your grandparents. For that matter you'll be lucky to make it out of Riverdale. If the blast doesn't get you the radioactive fallout will kill you, most likely."

"But that's why we have these shelters," Bobby shot back. His family had one. "That's why we bought these things, so we'd be safe."

"Safe?" Ian asked. I admired him, the way he could challenge these eighth graders. He couldn't play sports with them — they would never have let him in our games after lunch at school — but he wasn't shy about taking them on, out-talking them, proving that he knew more than they did. "It won't be safe for months, in some places it won't really be safe for at least a year. Don't fool yourselves. One way or another it'll spread out everywhere, and kill us."

"That's a lot of bull!" a voice shouted. "Who's going to get killed?"

And then Mike, a few rows behind us, was shouting at Ian. "Don't give us this radioactive crap, Gilbert! That's not gonna kill everybody! Maybe New York City'll get it. Or Washington, if they want to try to wipe out the President and all. Big deal! Who's gonna shoot a little town in Connecticut? You guys must be paranoid!"

Few of us knew the word. Mike could see the blank expressions on our faces. "Yeah, paranoid," he said, again, as the bus slowed down to pick up the group at the corner of Orchard and Bayberry. "It means you're chicken!"

Mike's accusation was too much for a couple of guys in the back.

"Chicken my ass!" several of them shouted. Jeff Connors was one of them. He came up the aisle even as six people from the Orchard Street stop, including Gary Campbell, got on and looked for a seat. Jeff blocked their way as he leaned over and pointed a finger in Mike's face: "Chicken hey? We'll kill those bastards! Have we ever lost a war? Well, there's no way we're gonna lose this one either. Just wait!"

"Hey, let's clear the way back there, Connors!" shouted Alice, our bus driver, as she shifted the bus, uneasily, into first gear.

After we lurched forward Gary took Jeff by the shoulders and guided him towards the back, saying, "Keep cool boy!" I was surprised at how easily Jeff seemed to give in. Gary knew we were all watching. "Not going to lose, hey?" he announced. "Like you and the Bears weren't supposed to lose to us last night, right, Connors? Gee, what was the score? Lions, 42, Bears, let's see — 12? Talk about getting killed!" And he gave Jeff a friendly punch in the back.

The loudest talk soon turned to football. Ian and I said little the rest of the ride over to school. He mumbled some things about "a bunch of morons," but I looked out my window most of the way. Pumpkins, most of them still smooth and faceless, sat on the front porches of many homes. And I looked up: the sun was rising over the trees to the east, and even though the winds on Sunday had sent many of the leaves to the ground, those trees were still full of color. It was a beautiful morning.

Mr. Reynolds struck me as a new man. He wore a dark brown tweed jacket that fit him well, a brighter tie than usual — navy blue with gold stripes, and light gray pants that looked newly pressed. I also noticed an unusual bounce to his step as he marched from the back of the room to the front. For a teacher who was never too friendly, he even seemed pleased to see us.

He approached the board with his *New York Times* in his left hand. He hurriedly wrote "1, 2, 3, 4, 5, 6, 7" from top to bottom, and then began to list the seven steps of action the President had outlined the previous evening, stabbing at the board in his fierce print, with his capital letters slanting in numerous directions:

1. QUARANTINE ON OFFENSIVE MILITARY EQUIPMENT — INCREASED SURVEILLANCE
2. FURTHER ACTION IF BUILD-UP CONTINUES
3. NUCLEAR MISSILE LAUNCHED FROM CUBA — AN ATTACK BY U.S.S.R., REQUIRING FULL RESPONSE

And so on. When he finished he took a fast attendance check, and then he took a few steps out in front of his desk to show us the headline, the three rows, all in large black capital letters, that marched across the top of page one. There was a photograph of Kennedy giving the speech from his desk in the Oval Office. Mr. Reynolds turned the paper around and began to read.

U.S. IMPOSES ARMS BLOCKADE ON CUBA ON FINDING OFFENSIVE MISSILE SITES; KENNEDY READY FOR SOVIET SHOWDOWN

"And other headlines," Mr. Reynolds continued.

*Ships Must Stop/ Other Action Planned
If Big Rockets Are Not Dismounted*

*President Grave/ Asserts Russians Lied
And Put Hemisphere In Great Danger*

He looked up at us. "Here are the first two sentences by James Reston:

> President Kennedy drew the line tonight, not with Cuba, but with the Soviet Union. After almost a generation of trying to keep the 'cold war' from reaching a direct

Tuesday, October 23

confrontation between United States and Soviet power, a decision has been made to force Soviet missile bases from this hemisphere at the risk of war.

So," Mr. Reynolds said, putting the paper down, "how many of you saw the President last night?"

Almost half of us raised our hands.

"Good. Well here's the situation." And he proceeded to explain the seven "initial" steps that he had summarized on the board. Mr. Reynolds spoke enthusiastically. "The lessons of history are clear," he said, "as the President pointed out last night: 'aggressive conduct, if allowed to go unchecked and unchallenged, ultimately leads to war.' So we check it now, or invade. But we do not simply sit idly by. It's about time, if you ask me."

Still, he had his doubts. He came out to the front row.

"A number of questions, of course, are still being asked, that we'll be asking in the hours and days ahead. Most obvious, of course, is: will this be enough? To choose a blockade rather than an invasion, has the President gone far enough to force the Soviets to stop? What follows if these 'initial' steps don't work? We now know they have these offensive weapons nearly ready to use. How long does Cuba, or Russia, let them sit there, in a crisis, without being tempted to use them?"

I was lost. Mr. Reynolds was asking too much of us, too much of me, anyway. But I looked over at Ian, who seemed to be following every word. His face did not have his customary scowl, nor was he pretending not to listen. Instead, his lips curled in, and his eyes narrowed. I realized he was getting angry.

"This blockade," Mr. Reynolds continued, walking to his left, towards the tall windows, "while clearly a step in the right direction, might not be enough to make us safe. It certainly won't remove Castro and the Communists from the hemis—"

"*What's safe?*" It was Ian. His voice was different than it had been on the bus; it was close to a scream. His head was shaking. He stood up, not as if he wanted to speak to the class — but as if he wanted to leave. I couldn't believe it. He was walking towards the door. "What's safe about bombing Cuba? We'll just get wiped out when they retaliate, that's all! What's *safe* about that!"

"Gilbert, you wait right there!" Mr. Reynolds was hurrying across the front of the room, but Ian had begun to run.

"Leave me alone!" he yelled, and he ran out the door, and we could hear him taking the stairs on our left two steps at a time, his loafers making a clear "tap, tap, tap" sound, six times, then he was on the landing, his feet scuffling as he approached the big door, then he opened it, "Bang!" — and he was outside. And then we heard that heavy door come to a close, hesitantly, with a last metallic, two-part, "Cl-lunk."

We never spoke to teachers this way. I waited for Mr. Reynolds to explode. Instead, he smiled a little.

"Liberal courage," he said, with a chuckle. He looked towards the hallway, for a moment. There was only silence. Then he continued.

"Well, as I was saying—," and he returned to his thoughts on whether the President's actions would be enough.

We heard three more reports that morning, but with five minutes left in class Mr. Reynolds spoke to us again about the Soviet missiles in Cuba. He walked along the aisle to our right, in front of the windows. I could peek through the yellow and gold of the maple trees now, in places, and see South Street, and cars passing by. Mr. Reynolds spoke to us in an unusually soft tone of voice.

"Have to admit, as a teacher, moments like this make it worthwhile. Maybe this helps you see the value of history, of social studies, of all we've been trying to do. My bet is you understand some of what is happening better than most seventh graders in this country. Hope you take some pride in that, because I do. Now, of course, we really need to pay attention. These are interesting times. So that's your homework this week: read the paper, listen to the news, talk with your parents. It is good you understand what's going on here.

"Who knows," he added, "maybe some of you will remember this week the way your parents and I can recall Pearl Harbor." The bell rang. Doors opened, voices grew in the hallway. Mr. Reynolds raised his voice for a final word. "So keep your eyes open, today and tomorrow and the next few days. Pay attention." And, for the first time that fall, he offered a warm smile. "See you tomorrow."

I went over to Ian's desk to get his books, and I brought them over to Math class, up the two flights of stairs in the Main Building. Ian was waiting outside the classroom with his head down.

"You all right?" I asked.

"OK," he said, taking his books. "Guess I'm in big trouble though, right?"

"He didn't seem too mad."

"Really?" he asked. I nodded. He looked slightly relieved. "I can't believe I did that." Then his eyes narrowed and I could tell he was still sore about it, and he said, "God, he's such a jerk!" We headed in to class and took our seats.

My father wasn't worried. Mr. Reynolds seemed pleased. How could this be? Over lunch, in the cafeteria, there was more talk of what we would do, or what might happen, if a war began, if a bomb were dropped in New York City. I ate quickly and went to the gym and sat down in the stands and read *Hiroshima*. The scenes were gross, but I kept reading. A man reached down to take a woman by her hands, "but her skin slipped off in huge, glovelike pieces." A minister went to offer a drink of water to a few soldiers. But then he discovered, as I read on:

> they were all in exactly the same nightmarish state: their faces were wholly burned, their eyesockets were hollow, the fluid from their melted eyes had run down their cheeks. (They must have had their faces upturned when the bomb went off; perhaps they were anti-aircraft personnel.) Their mouths were mere swollen, pus-covered wounds, which they could not bear to stretch enough to admit the spout of a teapot.

The bell rang for fifth period, and I headed off to French. Was Mr. Reynolds correct to see this simply as an "interesting time"? I was paying attention. Was he? What if Ian was right? What if none of us were safe?

And then we had our first drill.
It was 2:05 — we still had twenty-five minutes left in our last period, and Mr. Knapp, our science teacher, was in the middle of a talk on the cell and protoplasm, when the principal came over the loudspeaker — but without the usual

Tuesday, October 23   103

warning: the taps, the hum, the voices in the background, the class turning to look up. None of that. I was startled. The principal barged right in with four simple words, "I have an announcement."

Mr. Knapp put down his piece of chalk. I stared at the number he had written across the board at the beginning of class. Each individual number was over a foot tall. It told us when, according to scientists, cells first appeared.

3,000,000,000 YEARS AGO

The principal seemed to wait a long time for classes to stop and listen. At last he continued.

"Will all students please return to their homerooms by 2:10," he stated, evenly. "Teachers, please dismiss your classes in one minute, and be ready to meet with your homeroom classes at 2:10, as instructed. Thank you." Click.

What could we possibly have to discuss for twenty minutes? Student Council elections were over. The December Fair was still six weeks away.

But no one complained. Mr. Knapp asked us to write down our assignment for the next day, six pages of reading from our textbook. And then, rather stiffly, I thought, he said, "OK, move along now, do not linger, go directly to your homeroom." We headed out the door. There was a buzz of excitement: what could this sudden change in the schedule mean? It was fun, it was different. My science class was on the second floor of the Annex, so I had to weave my way through two flights of crowded stairways to get to Mrs. Brady and homeroom. I hurried down.

Mrs. Brady sat at her desk. The collars of her pink shirt fell out of her soft red sweater, catching the end of her shoulder length blond hair. She looked out at the twenty-seven of us without her usual good humor. She did not smile, or even speak at all, for some time. Every chair was full, I noticed, so there was no need to check attendance. Why did she hesitate?

Above us the pipes let out the occasional "clink" and "hiss-s-s-s," but it wasn't a racket, the non-stop drumming it had been some mornings. Mrs. Brady left her desk and went over and closed the classroom door. Her hair seemed especially bright and shiny that day. Lynn told me all the girls envied Mrs. Brady for her beautiful hair. I found myself following her legs, in moments like this, when I knew she wasn't looking. She wore low heels most days. That day they were a light khaki, matching the color of her skirt.

Then she turned, but her eyes looked beyond us. She made her way along the left side of the room toward the back windows, and closed them. This was a little odd, I thought; Jerry and Mike usually took care of the windows. She looked worried, but when I found myself staring too curiously I pulled my eyes away. I looked over at Kitty. She was whispering to the girl beside her, whispering the way she always did just before breaking into long, helpless giggles. I then glanced up at the clock. 2:12. Kitty giggled out loud.

"Quiet!" Mrs. Brady said, sternly.

Her heels clipped their way around the back of the room, around Cindy's desk in the corner, and then up along the right hand side. Once she was back in front of the room she turned and looked at us. The words finally came.

"We are going to have a drill—," she began, trying to sound as certain as possible. She moved behind her desk,

Tuesday, October 23

placing her palms down, and leaned forward. "—and so I want you to listen very carefully."

We tucked our chairs in a few inches, sat up a little straighter, and stopped fiddling with our pens and pencils.

"In a few minutes the bell will ring almost exactly as it does when there's a fire alarm. However, I am told it is going to be a little different. Because it is not for a fire alarm." She paused. Her voice, usually so calm, shook enough for me to notice. I looked around to see if I was the only one puzzled by her strangely mechanical delivery. But she had more to say.

"This drill," she continued, "is for the possibility of a nuclear attack. This building, this basement, will serve as a fallout shelter, at least for now. You all know about the atomic bomb and fallout, I'm sure, from your families and from TV, or maybe from school."

Not from school, I thought, immediately. Not in my case. Not until this moment.

Now that silence was broken. Now it was official.

Mrs. Brady went on. "You know that an atomic bomb is a terrible thing and spreads over a wide distance. And you know that Russia is not our friend and that she has these bombs. And now maybe Cuba does, too. Or will." She hesitated. She still sounded unconvinced of her own words, I thought, but after a moment she went on. "It is almost unimaginable," she insisted, "to think that Russia and the United States could ever go to war. But the school system has asked us to practice a certain drill in case of an alert. In case, they tell us, in case of a nuclear attack. And so we will."

Her rhythm picked up as she began to give directions. We half listened. We were still trying to absorb what she had just told us. For all our wild talk that morning on the bus, and over lunch, here was proof that the bomb was no myth, no fantasy.

The bomb was real.

And now we were about to learn how to protect ourselves against the fallout.

Something else was also possible, I thought. It was very possible that God would not let it happen.

I tried to recall the passages from the Bible Mr. Saarinen had assigned in the spring, about wars and rumors of wars. I could not remember if Christ said they would come as an early warning of His return, along with those other signs, or if they would take place almost at the moment He appeared, descending on the clouds of heaven....

Judgment Day. That was possible, too. That was preferable, in fact, wasn't it? Better Christ's coming again in judgment than what Mrs. Brady was now suggesting might happen — little Hiroshimas all over the world.

No, God would not let such a thing take place.

I realized that Mrs. Brady was staring at me, or so I thought, as if to bring me back to her words. I nodded, and paid attention again.

"—so when the bell rings," she directed, "you will line up the same way you do for a fire alarm, no running, no pushing, but quickly with no talking. You'll move toward the door. I have taken care of the windows so Jerry and Mike," she looked beyond me to the back row, "you won't need to do that this time. When you have lined up I will—," but just then she was interrupted. The click and hum of the loudspeaker were obvious this time. Then we heard a shuffle of papers and a brief, mumbled conversation. Mrs. Brady stood still and we all listened as the principal spoke.

"Teachers should have their classes prepared. The alarm will sound in one minute." Another click, and the hum ended.

Mrs. Brady moved closer to us as our eyes — hers, too — shot up to the clock on the wall. 2:15. We watched the second hand and silently started counting down: 57-56-55-54.... As we did in preparing for a fire alarm, some of us had already turned sideways in our chairs, facing to the left, left hand on the back of the chair, ready to stand up and push the chair in in one motion, ready to bolt to the front of the line. Still, our eyes were drawn to our teacher. For the next fifty seconds her command over us was absolute. She hurried over to the side wall, and, turning her back to it, began:

"OK, so you'll line up, then go out to your left — not to your right, not outside, but to your left. Then you will sit along the side of the wall out here to your left," she said, bending down and sitting on the floor herself, her back against the wall. "You will have to bring your knees up to your chin and then tuck your head down between your knees — like this." She demonstrated, ducking her face down, leaving us only her blond hair to look at. She held her knees tight together. We could see some of her white slip. I forced my eyes to stay off that slip to look up at her blond hair; I thought it was the polite thing to do. After a second or two she reappeared. She nodded to her hands still holding on to her ankles. "You will be able to hold your knees up if you grab your ankle this way; then just pull them in as close as you can. And remember, above all, keep your head down the entire time. No looking around."

She stood up, lifted her hair back behind her ears, and dusted off the back of her skirt.

"Any questions?" she asked.

The room was silent. She began to walk toward her desk to pick up her pocketbook.

"We are told," she said, less firmly now, as she pulled her pocketbook's long strap over her right shoulder, "that this is how you will be safest—," but she paused, looked down, twisted and untwisted the strap under her shoulder, before finishing, "—safest if there were, if something like this did happen to take place."

She began a weak smile, but then stopped.

Our minute was nearly over. Mrs. Brady's eyes joined ours as we studied the remaining jumps of the second hand. As she stepped toward the door the countdown ended ... 4-3-2-1. She grabbed the doorknob as the short blasts — *"Nnnnn! Nnnnn! Nnnnn!"* — began. It was startling how loud they were. Why, I wondered? To reach the gym classes way out on the fields? I wanted to cover my ears. *"Nnnnn! Nnnnn! Nnnnn!"* Hard, quick notes, so unlike the continuous clanging ring for the fire alarm, so demanding, driving us out, now! now! quick! run! hide! — *"Nnnnn! Nnnnn! Nnnnn! Nnnnn! Nnnnn!"*

We scrambled out of our chairs into line. I thought of some World War II movies I had seen on TV, where everyone was running for shelter — in London, I assumed. The siren here at school reminded me of the piercing wail of those air raids, their warning that the Nazi bombers were on their way, their urgent cry to run faster, to hurry into the cellars, the subway stations, as far down as they could go.

We were running now, too, in spite of Mrs. Brady's reminders to "Walk!" Once in line she gave us a look of,

Tuesday, October 23

"Now let's do this right," and then she opened the classroom door. We turned left and proceeded down the hallway, up to the spot where another class had already started to sit. Then we, too, dropped down against the wall and onto that cement floor, painted "battleship gray," as Ian had once told me, and brought our knees up and sank our heads between them, hoping to hold them there, as best we could, for five long minutes.

Five minutes for me to stare inside the darkness under my legs and study the U.S. Keds stickers on the back of my sneakers, to follow the cracks in the gray paint along that cold cement floor. Five minutes to smell the boys' locker room stench that filtered out into the hallway, making me think of Friday's game, of the touchdown pass I had caught, of the one good open field tackle I had made. Five minutes to wonder where Lynn's class would be, and where Debbie would be.

And then it struck me that there was something familiar about this ... and I suddenly recalled those days back in third or fourth grade, when we had ducked our heads under our desks, huddling down there.... How could I have forgotten? But now I remembered, too, that back then I had played jacks with the boy and the girl beside me during the drill, if that is what it was, when our teacher left the room. I had no idea what those exercises were all about. No one discussed U.S.-Soviet relations with us then, at eight or nine years old. We just ducked. And played. And waited.

But now it was different. I was no longer unaware of the Cold War behind this drill. I knew enough now to have some idea of what it meant.

I took in all I heard and felt around me. I was trying to pay attention, as Mr. Reynolds had asked us to do. The short blasts, "*Nnnnn! Nnnnn! Nnnnn!*", had stopped. Above me I could hear the quiet rumble of other classes still descending the stairs to reach the basement floor. Some classes went off into the gym to sit. "Against the far wall, remember!" a teacher shouted. I heard the voices of other teachers, including the sharp barking of Mr. Reynolds himself, as he came down with his homeroom class, all of their voices directing students: "Over here," "This way"; counting out loud — "... twenty-three, twenty-four, twenty-five — yes, all here"; scolding someone for talking; speaking more softly once every class had made it downstairs, almost whispering. When we had all folded our bodies up on that basement floor and had bowed our heads, our teachers still paced. Their footsteps only grew louder.

I heard Mrs. Brady's heels approach. I imagined her light khaki heels and her lightly tanned legs walking slowly in front of our twenty-seven pairs of bucks and loafers and sneakers. Occasionally an uneasy whisper, "Mike, ssshhh," or, "Kitty, keep your head down!" made me want to look up. Mrs. Brady's legs were beside me. She was standing still. Now the only sound was Cindy sniffling.

I was not surprised. It did not sound like the hysterical sobs we had heard and seen back in sixth grade, when John Glenn had lifted off into outer space. She muffled her sobs now. And yet I knew — all of us knew, I suppose, without looking up — that it had to be her.

Even so, I wanted to look. I pulled my chin up just a little and took a quick glance at her. Mrs. Brady stepped over to her side, but she did not reach out her hand, or bend over to comfort Cindy. I saw that Cindy's head was above her knees. She had taken her glasses off. Her right ear was pressed against one knee, and her head was turned sideways,

Tuesday, October 23 111

awkwardly so, I thought; both eyes were wide open, and red, and full of tears, and her left hand kept rubbing away under her sniffling, runny nose. Her tears rolled sideways off her red cheeks onto that gray basement floor.

At last those five minutes came to an end. We were allowed to lift our heads. I tried to take a deep breath, but I could not. I felt as if there were something stuck in my throat, or in my chest. It was like the feeling I had when I tried to eat a peanut butter and jelly sandwich too quickly. I gave Cindy another curious look, as did many of my classmates. But for once not one of us, not even Kevin or Mike or Jerry, wanted to tease her for her tears; no one even whispered, "Hey, Goofy!" We said little. We walked back in to class, sat down at our desks, and waited for the 2:30 bell, or for Mrs. Brady's return, to break this silence, the strange reserve we were feeling.

The classroom door opened and Mrs. Brady stepped in. She walked over to her desk and sat down. She folded her hands and looked up.

"You did fairly well for your first try," she said. "Just remember not to run, there is no need to panic," and she smiled, as if speaking to us again about a fire drill, but immediately she lost her smile, and looked down. She cleared her throat. "The principal asked us to remind you," she continued, her chin rising, her eyes looking beyond us now, I thought, "not to open your eyes at all during such drills. Keep your heads down between your knees; there's a reason for it, we are told. Oh yes, and don't look out the window," her voice seemed hurried now, "we are supposed to tell you this, too, if you're in another class, and there is a window to the west, toward New York, that way—," she said, pointing behind her, "—facing South Street, when, uh, the drill begins, don't look up." I felt I had some idea of what she must be talking about, but she rushed through these words as if they hardly mattered. "Anyway, pretty good. I understand we will have more drills during the next few days, so we will try to do even better the next time."

Then she stared at the top of her desk for a moment, took out some papers from one of her French classes, and started to grade them. I still found it hard to take a deep breath. I practiced taking short breaths, until the class ended.

When the 2:30 bell rang most of us headed straight for the door. I took my time leaving. I thought Mrs. Brady might want to talk with me for a moment, as she sometimes did at the end of homeroom. But as I drifted by her desk, and then stepped slowly toward the door, she never looked up. I went out, taking a quick look back. Only Cindy was left. She was in her chair in the far corner, with her head now cradled in her arms, on her desk. She was still crying.

My father had told me to take the day off. He had a meeting at the newspaper at 4 p.m. to place an ad for winter sports equipment, and he said it might run late. So I took the bus home. Lynn was alone in her seat, and I joined her. She did not seem to mind.

We talked about the drill for a minute. She had to do the same thing in the basement of the Main Building.

"They couldn't fit us all in the hallway, some of us had to be in the cafeteria, and the floor smelled of ammonia. Two girls almost fainted! I felt a little sick myself. And my skirt got all dirty. It was terrible! I can't believe they're going to

Tuesday, October 23

make us do it again tomorrow." I didn't say anything. And then, more slowly, she added: "I can't believe this whole thing. Can you?"

"No," I said. "Mrs. Brady, I don't think she likes it either," I told her. "And Cindy cried. A lot."

"So, can you blame her? I was ready to cry, too."

At home we gathered around the kitchen table. My mother had taken the ironing board from out of the pantry and was ironing our clothes there beside the stove. Lynn folded the laundry and created three piles on the kitchen table: one for Danny and me, one for Beth and her, one for Mom and Dad. The rest of us took out some ice cream and cookies and had a snack. My mother listened to our stories. Beth and Danny had also practiced a drill at West School. Beth said she saw Danny down the hallway, with his first-grade class, when she and her fourth-grade classmates came into the corridor during the drill.

"I see him, all tucked up, his hands on his ankles, in the right position, but then—," Beth grew excited as she came to this part, "but then he rolls right across the hall, in a little ball, the stupid idiot, right when everyone was getting quiet and all!"

"Danny!" my mother said, in surprise. I caught Lynn's eyes as she looked over at me; she was ready to break out laughing, but she was covering her mouth so as not to show it. Soon I was laughing, too.

"I couldn't help it!" Danny protested. "I tucked up and go like this — look, it's easy!," and he squatted down on the kitchen floor and started his forward roll, rolling from the refrigerator right across the room until he bumped into the dishwasher, and all of us laughed, which encouraged him to tuck himself up again and roll right on back.

After supper I went upstairs to my room. Passing by Lynn and Beth's room I heard their voices, and their radio. The funny new song, "Monster Mash," was playing. I wanted to hear the words, and knocked and went in.

"Oh, good," Lynn said, "Tommy, maybe you'll know." Both Lynn and Beth were on their beds. I saw the book Lynn was reading for school, *The Diary of Anne Frank*, sitting under her bedside lamp. "Do you know how much time for radiation to spread from New York City? I told Beth five minutes, if they dropped the bomb in New York, we'd have five minutes."

"I don't know." I moved over between their two beds. Lynn had her Algebra I book and her notebook open at the foot of her bed. I thought of Ian's words on the bus that morning, and of what I could guess from my reading of *Hiroshima*. But that was different: that bomb was dropped not far from the center of the city. New York was an hour away by car. Would it travel that fast — 60 miles per hour? Or faster than that?

"A little more than that, I bet," I said. "I don't know. It would have to come fifty miles or so, remember."

"What would?" Beth asked.

"The radiation," I answered.

Beth looked puzzled, and asked again, "So, will we come home?"

"What do you mean?" I asked.

"If it happens while we're in school, could we get on the school bus, wouldn't they send us home?"

I looked at Lynn and shrugged. I realized I should say what Beth would want to hear.

"Yes, probably, they'd probably take us home, if they knew they had the time. If we're in school—," I began, but just then it hit me, too, for the first time ... we might have to stay there for days, or weeks ... and I stopped.

"Oh my gosh!" Lynn's right hand came up to her mouth for a moment. "I just thought of something." She immediately put her feet on the floor and began to get her shoes on.

"What is it?" Beth asked.

"Have either of you checked the cellar?" she asked.

I shook my head.

"What for?" Beth said.

"For how we'd live down there, in case of a bomb. You know. Remember we put some soup and some other stuff down there, I don't know, two years ago. Remember?"

In a minute we were following her through the door to the cellar. She turned on the lights. After reading most of *Hiroshima*, where so much of the city had been buried under rubble and where so many fires had destroyed one building after another, cellars and bomb shelters now made some sense to me. And yet I read of people screaming for help from out of the bottom of their ruined houses, some buried alive, there being no way, or no one, to help.... If this old stone house of ours collapsed, I thought, we, too, might be buried alive.

We spent five minutes looking it over. We studied the two small windows that opened just above the ground and noticed cracks in the stone walls. We tracked down the source of the foul smell: three dead mice. The ancient furnace seemed to be leaking oil. Our investigation assured us this would not be safe. "Our teacher said you *really* have to be underground," Lynn said, "in a cellar that is well sealed from possible fallout. This isn't."

"What do you think?" I asked her.

"I think we ask Mom and Dad to get a bomb shelter, that's what."

"But you know Dad wouldn't get one before."

"Well, then," she looked at both Beth and me knowingly, as if this was one of those times when we would have to go around our father, "we'll ask Mom. We've got to do something! I'm not going to live down here, are you?" Lynn swiped at some cobwebs just above her head. "I'll say all of us want one, is that OK with you?"

Beth told her she should ask for one like the Auerbachs'. It had beds, and a little stove, and a toilet, with a curtain.

I did not say anything.

I knew, though, that I did not want to be at school when the bomb came. I wanted to be home.

> "Today the United Nations faces a moment of grave responsibility. What is at stake is not just the interests of the parties directly involved, nor just the interests of all Member States, but the very fate of mankind. If today the United Nations should prove itself ineffective, it may have proved itself so for all time."
>
> U Thant, Acting Secretary General of the United Nations speaking to the U.N. Security Council
> October 24, 1962

CHAPTER TEN

Wednesday, October 24

WEDNESDAY MORNING I WOKE UP around 6 a.m. I went downstairs to look at the paper. My father was in the library already, in his blue bathrobe, working. Three large black notebooks were spread out in front of him. He was often up early, that fall. When I drove home with him after work he usually had those notebooks with him — financial statements, he told me, that he needed to study.

He looked up.

"Hi boy," he said.

"Hi Dad." I stepped on to the threshold.

"A little early, isn't it?"

"Yeah, but I didn't think I could get back to sleep."

"Your mother's not feeling too well this morning," he said, taking a sip of his coffee, "I hope we didn't wake you?" I shook my head, no. "You feel OK?" he asked.

"I'm fine," I said. Actually I was a little tired. I had stayed up until 10 p.m. — neither of my parents had knocked and told me to turn off my light — and finished *Hiroshima*.

"You want to help me go over the books?" he said, with a grin. I shook my head, and tried to smile in return. I looked to see if he had the *Times* by his chair. He understood.

"I left the paper in the kitchen," he said. "I think the Knicks lost."

"Thanks." I turned to go.

"Come join me if you want."

I reached the kitchen, poured a glass of orange juice, and brought the paper back out to the library. I sat down in the small sofa my mother used, across the room from my father.

The headline again ran across the top of page one. It read:

SOVIET CHALLENGES U.S. RIGHT TO BLOCKADE; INTERCEPTION OF 25 RUSSIAN SHIPS ORDERED; CUBA QUARANTINE BACKED BY UNITED O.A.S.

There was a photograph, too, just under the headline, offering proof, the caption told me, of the missile site in Cuba. It described what I was looking at — I couldn't see very much myself — as "a typical surface-to-air missile base, with indi-

Wednesday, October 24

cations of facilities under construction and anti-aircraft weapons."

I read two smaller headlines:

VESSELS SPOTTED

*McNamara Says Navy
Will Make Contact
Within 24 Hours*

And the other:

MOSCOW REPLIES

*It Warns Washington
Action By Navy
Risks Nuclear Conflict*

I tried to read the first few paragraphs of these articles. My eyes kept going back to the headlines. The reading was difficult.

"Nikita doesn't seem to get the picture quite yet," my father said.

I looked up.

"Does it worry you?" he asked.

I nodded.

"What they're asking you to do in school, I don't know if that's right — I think it's nuts myself — but Tommy, please don't let it get to you. Those drills are designed mostly to please some bureaucrat, some idiot in the civil defense department. This thing could get bigger, granted, but it's absurd to think we're in any danger here. Please believe that."

I did not say anything. I did not want my father to realize how afraid I was. But I also felt that he would not understand.

He got up, taking his glazed, navy-blue coffee mug with him. He came over and gave my head a rub. "Don't forget the sports pages. They're more fun." And he left.

I leafed through the rest of the paper. My eyes fell on an article about how New Yorkers were coping with the crisis. Many kept their sense of humor, it said. A few couples or friends were now using "a cute phrase" when they said goodbye: "See you later, if at all."

Before leaving for school I went in to see my mother. The shades were still down. She was watching Dave Garroway and the "Today" program. I walked around my father's unmade bed and stepped up beside my mother. She said she felt pretty good, and that she would be up soon.

"I hope you feel better, Mom."

She gave me a kiss and a warm hug.

"See you later," she said.

I returned *Hiroshima* to Cindy that morning in homeroom, and thanked her.

"It's terrible," I said. "Unbelievable."

"I'm glad you read it," she told me.

"Hope your talk goes well," I said, heading for my chair.

She seemed surprised. "Thanks," she said, brightening. "Thanks. You too."

Mrs. Brady passed out a piece of paper, telling us that the town of Riverdale wanted us to take these sheets home to our parents. At the top of the page it said: "To Remember in Case of an Emergency," and at the bottom of the page it was signed, "The Civil Defense Commission." It was simply a list of items to keep "in your shelter," as it said near the top of the page. The list included:

first-aid kit
fire extinguisher
flashlight
batteries
candles
gas stove
matches
water
shovel/pick

Water. I could not forget the description of those men and women in Hiroshima, who could not even open what was left of their mouths.
I put the list in my hip pocket.

Mr. Reynolds again seemed eager to talk about the headlines and the latest news, even though we were supposed to hear Cindy and Jerry, and maybe Michelle, too, give their U.N. reports. It occurred to me that we might not get to my talk on Berlin for several days.

"Some exaggerate what America is trying to do here," Mr. Reynolds was saying, as he paced the front of the room. "We're not taking a great risk, and we're not being terribly aggressive. Maybe we'll need to take the next step, who knows. For now we're just telling the Soviets to stop breaking the Monroe Doctrine, which you know about. And not to threaten our national security. That's all." He looked Ian's way, before continuing. "We've challenged the Communists before, in Berlin in 1948, and in Korea. When your enemy puts nuclear weapons ninety miles from your shore, you damned well *better* be prepared to challenge them again."

He continued to move back and forth across the front of the room.

"This is a necessary challenge. If it becomes a war, it will be a necessary war. But some of this talk the last two days — and Gilbert—," and now he stared at Ian, and I turned and saw Ian's back straighten, his chin come up cautiously, and his eyes return Mr. Reynolds' stare, "—Gilbert, your little outburst yesterday was one example of such talk; talk of nuclear annihilation and so on exaggerates the situation. It's foolish."

He took a few steps back towards the middle of the room.

"I respect the fact that we provide these little drills here in school. They're of educational value. They may wake you up, to a number of things. And teach discipline. But chances that we're on the verge of a nuclear war are nill. Zip. Not with our nuclear superiority. If war is necessary, if Khrushchev and Castro won't cooperate, we send an air strike to take out those missiles. Or invade the island, as we tried to do over a year ago. Both are done with conventional weapons. Do you understand this?" Once more he looked over to Ian's row, before checking on all of us.

No, I did not understand this. His confidence seemed wrong, somehow. How could he be so sure?

And hadn't President Kennedy said something very different?

Then Mr. Reynolds gave us another rare smile, as he added, "So, as your saying goes, 'Keep *cool*, boy.'" And he raised both hands into the air and snapped his fingers.

He looked directly at Ian. I did too. I could see that Ian was trying not to laugh. A couple of guys couldn't hold it back, but Mr. Reynolds stared them down.

"Do you follow me Mr. Gilbert?"

Ian's half-smile had become a frown. He hunched his shoulders up — they seemed to tighten there at the back of his neck — and then he let them sag, and he offered a quick little nod of the head.

"Good," Mr. Reynolds announced. "So, Miss Mellum, you begin today."

I forgot about Ian. I tucked my chair in and sat up a little more. The whole class was anxious to see how Cindy would do. I wasn't the only one who wondered if she might not grow flustered, and turn red, and walk away. I hoped she could get through it.

Cindy gave us a brief history of the use of nuclear weapons, of the men who created the atomic bomb, and of their first explosion, "the Trinity test." She spoke of the two bombs that followed: the uranium bomb on Hiroshima, and the more powerful plutonium one at Nagasaki. "Two thirds of Hiroshima was destroyed," she told us, "and one half of

Nagasaki." Then she went on to outline the history of nuclear testing since World War II by the United States, and by the Russians, too, ever since 1949, when their first atomic bomb was tested. She said that both countries had begun to test again, and not just underground, in the past year.

Cindy spoke quickly, but she was very clear. At first her body was quite stiff; after a couple of minutes, though, she began to use her hands as she talked. I could feel the genuine concern in her words. I felt she wanted to teach us something. She reminded me, briefly, of Mrs. Schwartz.

"Why is a nuclear test ban so important?" she asked. She began to explain "what we know to be just some of the potential damage of what these weapons can do to people, based on Hiroshima and Nagasaki." And she spent several minutes retelling some of the grim facts found in *Hiroshima.*

"These bombs, remember, were small in comparison to today's thermonuclear bombs. The bomb that the Russians exploded in a test last year would have been 2,500 times more destructive than the bomb dropped on Hiroshima. And once they explode — even if they're set off on a deserted island in the Pacific Ocean — they send fallout into the stratosphere that then spreads around the world."

Then she tried to describe the delayed effects of radioactive fallout.

"There are several stages of radiation disease," she said. Her voice grew more emotional, her words more choppy. "Rays destroy body cells. This leads to hair falling out, fever, blood disorders, a loss of white blood cells. This can lead to a loss of red blood cells. This can lead to infections and tumors, and to diseases that last for months — or until a patient dies. For some who live, it means a problem," and here she blushed, but she looked determined, too, to say it, "a problem with your reproductive organs — so you can't have children. Or, as with many women of Hiroshima, after the war, where your babies aren't normal."

In her conclusion, she said there were "many good reasons, then, why we ought to stop testing and poisoning the air we breathe." As she finished, she glanced at Mr. Reynolds, standing over near Ian. Mr. Reynolds simply nodded and said, "Well researched. Well done." It bothered me that he didn't congratulate her further, or at least say a little more.... Cindy headed back to her seat. She seemed relieved, but she did not smile. I knew I would have smiled, I would have been very proud, if I could have given a talk like that. I knew now why my mother had been so impressed.

The class was silent. No matter how strange Cindy might seem at times, we had been reminded how very bright she was. And for those of us who had known her since fourth or fifth grade, we knew what a miracle it was, not only that she had finished her talk, but that — as it certainly appeared — she had actually *wanted* to give that speech.

"I would want to add," Mr. Reynolds began, walking towards the front of the room, but just then the short blasts boomed over the speakers and through the school — *"Nnnnn! Nnnnn! Nnnnn!"* We jumped, and bolted for the door. Almost all of us ran. A couple of chairs were knocked over. Above all the noise Mr. Reynolds' voice thundered at us, "*Get back!* All of you, get *back* to your desks!"

We did so. Only Cindy had stayed in her seat.

Mr. Reynolds went over to the side of the room and closed the two enormous windows that were slightly open. The siren continued: *"Nnnnn! Nnnnn! Nnnnn!"* We should stay away from that glass, or any glass, when the bomb hit, I thought, recalling the man in Hiroshima who had been sitting up against a window when the bomb landed, and how the glass had splintered into a thousand pieces, right into his back. And beyond those windows, I realized, there in Room 106, beyond those maples, was New York City. I remembered Mrs. Brady's words: "Don't look up."

Mr. Reynolds was in front of us again. He put on his most military voice as he shouted out his words, competing with and pushing through the alarm, the repeated blasts, that seemed to be coming from all directions.

"Let's show some discipline this time! Now *walk* to the door, *walk* down the stairs, and *walk* to the hallway, and go up to the second door to the boy's locker room, on the right hand side. Sit down there, between those two doors to the locker room. With your mouths *shut*! You got it?"

We nodded, eager to be set free, but trying not to show how anxious we were.

"Step forward," he demanded.

Everyone except Cindy was soon in line at the door. Cindy just sat at her desk.

Mr. Reynolds was only ten feet away from her, so even with the shrill cry of the alarm he hardly needed to scream at her the way he did, calling out, "Let's *move it* young lady! Let's go!"

But she did not move. I could see that she was shaking. I knew he was not going to get her like this. Everyone stared. Some of the guys shouted, "Get over here, Goofy!" Jerry added, "Come on Mellum, don't sit there like a fool!"

I left the line and walked over to her desk.

"We have to go downstairs, Cindy."

She looked up. Her eyes were growing red.

"It's OK," I said, "come on."

I could hear Mr. Reynolds behind me, approaching the desk. I turned around and could see his anger, and so I said, "She's coming." And with that I heard her chair slide out. I looked at her. She gave me a sad half-smile. The tears were beginning to fall. We walked to the end of the line together.

"OK," Mr. Reynolds said, "go ahead."

We walked downstairs and headed for our spot between the two other classes. In passing Mrs. Brady, who was counting the students in her first-period French class, already sitting up against the wall, with their heads down, I said, quietly, "Hi. Mrs. Brady." She looked up, but she did not turn my way. There was a blank look in her eyes, as if I weren't even there. As if none of us were there.

I sat down beside Cindy — I did not have much choice — and tucked my head inside my knees and tried to keep still for five minutes. I did not want to look up; I was afraid Cindy might be looking at me. She was silent. I heard no sobs, no sniffling.... The only noise came from above our heads as those pipes, at first hesitantly, and then more frequently, clinked and rattled and popped, almost like a gunshot — a hammering interrupted, once or twice, by a long, slow moan.

It was distracting, but with my head bowed, it seemed a good time to pray. I wondered why I hadn't prayed the day before, during those five minutes. But what should I ask for? If our life here was about to end, couldn't I ask Him to come back now? "Thy kingdom come, thy will be done...," yes, that was better than waiting for those bombs to fly.... Shouldn't I ask Christ to come save us, to appear in the sky and catch those missiles before they reached their target — New York,

Washington, ... and those going the other way — towards Moscow? In Mr. Saarinen's class I had read of a hell where there was "weeping and gnashing of teeth." In *Hiroshima* I had read of people with their eyes melting down their burned faces, just asking for a drink of water. If Christ must come, why not now, before it was too late?

But I could not pray for this. I could only say, "Please God, be with President Kennedy. And if it happens, please don't let it be while we're in school." And then, hardly thinking of the words, I mouthed the Twenty-third Psalm: "The Lord is my shepherd; I shall not want. He maketh me to lie down in green pastures. He leadeth me beside the still waters...."

The drill ended. We opened our eyes, stood up, dusted ourselves off, and headed back to class. I was now at the front of the line, Cindy right behind me. That second drill was less of a shock than the first. A couple of my classmates did not seem as subdued, as overwhelmed, as they had been the day before. Climbing the stairs I even heard some jokes behind me, about somebody's "secret weapon," as Jerry put it. "Come on, somebody has to take credit — who was it who produced that unbelievably foul odor? What a stink bomb that was!" And some eighth grader was holding an imaginary conversation with Khrushchev.

"You like this Nikita? You think we won't be ready? Wrong, you *nitwit*! Wait'll we bury *you*, you *asshole*!"

As we stepped back into the classroom I felt Cindy pat my back. I turned around. She was fumbling with her glasses with both hands, but then stopped and said, "Thanks Tom."

I nodded. I thought of her talk. "Your report — that was great Cindy. It was the best."

She smiled.

We gathered our books and prepared to go to second period. Mr. Reynolds asked to speak to Cindy as we were leaving. She remained in her chair, her eyes fixed straight ahead, as I headed for the door. It was the first time I felt angry at him.

Ian and I talked about Mr. Reynolds on the bus ride home.

"He's not the only one," Ian said. "It's all of them, practically. Adults — they think they're so smart. At least my parents aren't lying to me about all this," he said.

"What do they say?" I asked.

"Just what I said yesterday. That we're not likely to survive a war like this, our chances are one in a hundred, and we shouldn't expect any government — ours or theirs — to have the sense to realize this. My father just says, 'It's out of our hands,' and shrugs his shoulders. At least he doesn't pretend. Why, what do your parents tell you?"

I had no desire to defend my parents in front of Ian. I would probably lose, anyway.

"They tell me enough," I said.

Ian pulled down the window and half-stood to get his forehead and eyes up into the cool, fresh air. His blond hair lifted and shivered in the wind. He spoke now with his eyes closed. He seemed calm.

"Sometimes my dad talks of archaeologists finding our civilization, like we discovered other civilizations — you know, the Greeks and Romans and all. I don't know if he believes that. Maybe."

We had reached our stop. I waited for Lynn after getting off the bus, and then she and I moved up Bayberry Hill. Ian began to walk home along Woodside.

"See ya Ian," I said, to his back.

"See ya Tommy," he answered, with a half wave, without turning around.

The bus went by us and disappeared over the small rise near our driveway, and then reappeared again as it climbed the final hill of Bayberry. From that distance the yellow-orange of the bus matched the leaves along the roadside almost perfectly. But the trees were more bare every day. I could tell the difference even as Lynn and I walked home; she stepped away from the thicker piles of leaves, while I shuffled through them — my feet and ankles disappearing down there among all their many colors. Cars seeing us swerved halfway across the road. Some people gave us a friendly wave. Lynn, or I, waved back. It was fairly cool out, chillier than Monday or Tuesday. I thought I might shoot baskets for a while. Maybe, too, if my father came home at 5:30, just before dark, we could play catch with the football.

Lynn and I came in the first entrance to our driveway and walked up the semicircle to the front of the house. But we both heard loud noises — the growl of large machines, of heavy engines — not far away. Then I saw a truck on the other side of the driveway, near the turnaround. We both ran down to take a look.

There was another truck there, under the backboard. Out back, beyond the swings, to the right of the four apple trees, was a third truck, and a backhoe.

Lynn was the first to speak.

Wednesday, October 24

"What in the world! What's going on?"

We ran past the trucks, out among the four men who were watching as the backhoe roared and bounced, and as its arm scraped and rose and dumped another huge mouthful onto the bed of the truck. And behind that truck, there it was.

Next to the tall, wide evergreen stood an ugly looking structure of steel. As I looked at its rippled walls, and their semicircular shape, I counted them up ... twelve, thirteen, fourteen ridges or bumps. It was impossible not to think of a snail.

"Hello son!" the workers called out. "Hello young lady!" We waved. I wanted to ask, to be sure, but Lynn announced the news first.

"It's a bomb shelter!" she said, clapping her hands.

"I can see that," I insisted.

"Guess who is going to be *mad*!" she added, ignoring me, sounding both nervous and excited about the possibility of my parents having a fight.... Or had my father changed his mind? Was this something they had agreed on? But no, that very morning, once again, he had sounded so sure....

I stayed and watched for the next twenty minutes as the backhoe carved into the soil and filled its huge bucket with dirt. I had tried to dig in this same spot, once. Two years before I had decided to build a swimming pool. I told my parents I would dig it myself. They said sure, if I wanted to, go ahead. After a week of hard work, though, I had the feeling I was getting nowhere, and gave up. This backhoe took up more dirt in one scoop than I had shoveled out that entire week.

"We won't get done today," one of the men told me, when the backhoe paused for a moment. "But it'll be buried by tomorrow."

Soon my sweater did not feel warm enough, and I waved good-bye and went inside. I waited for the men and the trucks to leave before returning, this time with a light coat on, shortly after five o'clock. I could still see the sun just over the tops of the trees to the west. The shadows were long; the shadow of the bomb shelter stretched to the nearest apple tree, over forty feet away. I looked down in the hole, before seeking the door to the shelter. I had to jerk the heavy bar on the door several times before it would slide to the left. And then I walked in.

The room was completely empty, except for two pipes — five- or six-feet long, and shelves — lots of shelves. There were no beds. There was a small toilet; it reminded me of "the head" on the boats we had rented for our August cruises. This shelter was better than Randy's, but Beth was right: we would need a curtain. The steel walls were simply the reverse of what I had seen outside, rippled walls curving over my head. It felt colder all of a sudden. It reminded me of Eskimos in their igloos. I wondered how cold it would be, once we were underground.

I noticed two holes. For the pipes, I imagined. So we could get fresh air in the shelter? Really? And not breathe air that was radioactive? As it was, it smelled odd, a cold, steely smell, somehow both new and stale. I wondered what an igloo smelled like.

I noticed the many shelves again, too. I felt I ought to try to fill them up as soon as possible.

The room was smaller than my bedroom. Six of us would have to live here.

Wednesday, October 24   133

I left the shelter and walked over to the piles of soft dirt at the edge of the hole. Then I jumped in. The dirt was dry; the strong, pungent smell, the broken roots, the worms crawling all around me.... It made me think of Jody, in *The Yearling*. How well he knew the soil, out "hoein' the corn and the cow-peas," and the woods, with its sink-hole, and swamp, and all those wild animals.... It felt cool down here. The ground was more than a foot over my head. The walls of dirt around me seemed enormous and strong. Yes, a swimming pool would have been nice here.

I heard a car come in the driveway. I leaped into the air to see if it was my father. Yes, it was the gray VW. I ducked back down. I did not want to be caught here. I heard his car stop. Had he seen me? I could tell he had not yet made the turn in the driveway. I was afraid he might jump out of the VW and slam the car door shut and rush out to this new hole in his backyard — and find me. I waited. The car continued to idle. Finally I heard it shift into first gear, and it climbed the last eighty feet to its space behind Mom's Rambler. His car door closed, firmly.

I went to the nearest wall and tried to scramble out, but I slipped in the soft dirt on the edges. I felt as if I were trying to do chin ups on the bar in gym class, but I quickly realized this was quite different. My face and chest scraped hard against the dirt wall as I attempted my climb; my fingers couldn't get a good grip on the ground above me. I tried to pull myself up by grabbing a fistful of grass in each hand, but that didn't work either, and my sneakers kept slipping as I tried to dig into the wall to drive myself out. Twice, almost out, I fell back down. It made me mad, and a little nervous. At last I succeeded in escaping. I started to run for the cellar, shaking off some of the dirt all over my coat and pants as I went, spitting out some of the dirt in my mouth, too, and cleaning off my face. I did not want my father to see me coming from the hole, in case he was now on his way out for a better look. I only stopped running once I had made it through the garage, and beyond the stairs in the furnace room. I took off my coat and brushed away the dirt that had fallen inside my jacket onto my sweater. I sat down and waited to see if I was going to hear an argument above me.

After a few minutes I took a broom leaning in the corner and began sweeping the cellar floor. Maybe the bomb shelter would not be ready in time. But this wasn't safe, I knew that now. In the shelter, though, if it were ready in time, maybe there we could survive a little longer.

I pulled the list from The Civil Defense Commission out of my hip pocket. I began to think where I could find these items: *first-aid kit*, in the linen closet in the hallway just outside my parents' room; *fire extinguisher*, the left-hand closet in the front hallway; *candles*, there were candles in the highboy. Candles. In the dark. Like Tom Sawyer and Becky in the cave, I thought, out of food, and Tom trying to be brave. I stopped on *gas stove*, but then remembered — the pantry, with the sterno cans, used by my mother two or three times there in Riverdale when the power had gone out. And to cook during those cruises in late August. Gas stoves and sterno cans, I now recalled, were how Nana had managed to have warm meals back in Sandy Harbor, during those hurricanes years before.

I put the list back in my pocket. There were a few puddles in the room; I tried to sweep them dry. I attacked the cobwebs as well. I looked at the two windows. In the garage I found two bags of sand. Something to block out the radiation, I thought. I couldn't lift them, but I dragged each bag through the garage, through the furnace room, and left each one under a window. My father could lift them up, if it happened before the shelter was ready.... It was silent, above me, for almost an hour, until I heard a faint cry: "Supper's ready!" It was Lynn's voice.

I climbed the stairs and went into the kitchen. My father wasn't there yet. Lynn had done the cooking. She looked at me and almost shouted, "Where have you been? My gosh, Tommy, you're a mess!" I realized I needed to clean up before I had to answer a lot of questions.

By the time I returned, my father was in the room, in his chair, already buttering his potatoes. I was told my mother still wasn't feeling well. There was little talk as we sat together and ate our hamburgers, baked potatoes, and lima beans. Lynn and I exchanged knowing glances.

I was glad to be reading *The Yearling* again. As I lay on my bed that evening, though, from the other side of the wall behind me, my parents' voices grew louder.

I knew I was hearing more than I ought to. It was especially easy to hear what my father was saying.

"... You don't just order something for that kind of money without our talking about it!"

"We did talk about it, it's just that—," I heard my mother begin, but I could not make out the rest of her words.

"Jesus, Sarah," my father demanded, "how can that thing be any security, don't throw that at me! That's not security! The store is security, my work is security, the stocks, you and I, you and I, *we're* their security. Not that god-awful little room they want us to go hide in. You know I don't want any part of it!"

I heard my mother say something about "just being realistic," but at these words my father swore again, "Oh Christ!" he snapped, and I jumped back a little as I heard their bedroom door rush open and as he stormed by outside our door, his defiant footsteps shaking even our room, his ankles cracking, his deep, angry, close-mouthed breathing whistling through his nose as he headed for the stairs. Then I heard him pull at the stairway railing, causing it to squeak. I listened as he thumped down the steps, the money in his pockets jingling, before he took a few more heavy strides through the hallway to the library, and slammed the door shut.

Lynn's door opened. I could just barely hear her light footsteps as she dashed by to my parents' room.

Danny was waiting to be put to bed. But he had heard my father, too. He asked me to play a game of hockey, and I sat down on the floor — even though it was past his bedtime — and for twenty minutes we took turns trying to shoot the marble past each other's goalie. A little later, when everything seemed quiet again, I heard my mother's voice say, "Sweet dreams, dear," before my sister — more slowly now — passed by outside our door. No one came to say good-night to Danny. At 8:45 he climbed into his bed on his own, and fell asleep.

I read another forty-five minutes. Then I went in to say good-night to my mother. It was quite dark; she only had her bedside light on. She was lying on her bed, her head up, the *Times* resting in front of her, with a Bob Hope special on the TV. I recognized Lucille Ball and Bing Crosby. I wondered if my mother would let me stay.

"Still awake?" she asked, when she noticed me at the foot of her bed. I expected her to say something about why no one had come in to put me to bed at 9 p.m.

"You feel any better?" I asked.

"Getting there," she said. "Switch it to channel 2, would you? Earlier they said they might have a report tonight. Let's take a look." I turned the channel. There was Walter Cronkite.

"You can stay for a few minutes if you want, Tommy," she said.

I was not tired, and I thought Mr. Reynolds would be pleased. I sat down on the foot of my father's bed and watched. I recognized U Thant giving a speech, calling for a "voluntary" — he pronounced it, vo-lun'-ta-ry — "suspension" of both the blockade and the shipment of Soviet arms. Then Cronkite talked with a reporter at the U.N., with another at the White House, and then with a third at the Pentagon. I noticed the Pentagon reporter's use of the word "security." He spoke of "national security at a time like this," and of a "war-time security guidance system." It seemed to me that he must be using the word in a different way than my father had done, earlier, when he called the store, and his work, "security." The Riverdale Sports Shop, and the Pentagon; they had nothing in common. It was too complicated for me. It made no sense.

In his summary Cronkite spoke of the possibility of "hostile action" that could lead to "armed conflict," and of the "chances for negotiation." And then he signed off.

My mother asked me to turn back to "The Bob Hope Show."

I approached my mother for a kiss good-night. In the light there at her bedside I could see that her eyes looked unusually pink, as if she had been crying some time that evening. Her hair, most always pulled back so neatly, looked rumpled after her day in bed. She patted the side of the bed, asking me to sit down. I did.

"Please understand, Tommy, I didn't get that shelter to worry any of you. It's a precaution. It may not make you feel safer, although I hope it does. Lynn told me last night how you all felt. The truth is, as much as anything, I bought it to make *me* feel safer." She was pulling at her hair, all gathered on her right shoulder; she undid the snarls — and she soon looked more like herself. "It just seems common sense," she continued, "with New York nearby and all. If something happens — and please know I don't think it will — but if something happens, I just wanted to know that at least we will be as safe as we can possibly be."

She seemed to wait for a reply.

"Does it bother you — that we have one?"

"No, it's good," I said. "I hope it happens here."

"What's that?" She sat up a little more, and the *Times* fell off the other side of the bed.

Where would this get me?

"No, it doesn't bother me. The cellar isn't any good. I'll start to fill it up as soon as it's ready."

"That's nice of you, Tommy, but I can do most of that." She took my left hand in her right hand and held it, rubbing the top of my hand with her thumb. "Listen, dear, I just hope you don't *expect* this thing to happen. There's no more than one chance in a million we'll ever end up using that — that building. As they say, it's the most remote of possibilities, that's all."

Not that remote, Mom. I thought of Ian's words about adults. I wondered how he would judge my mother.

No, Mom, it was no longer such a "remote possibility."

Wednesday, October 24 139

I gave my mother a half-smile and nodded.

"Please sleep well, dear," she said, pulling me closer and giving me a kiss.

"You, too, Mom. Hope you feel better."

I could not go to sleep. I expected to hear my father return upstairs at any time. It was another half hour before he did so. He tried to be quiet, climbing the stairs; he didn't use the banister, but there was a muffled squeak on each step, and his bones snapped and cracked. He came up the hallway and stood a few feet away from the door to both his room, and to our room. Did he want to speak with me? Probably not. He opened his door, and I heard the TV go off. As they began to talk I could just barely tell which voice was my mother's, which my father's, they were so quiet and indistinct. But they kept talking. And they were still talking, the last I knew, before I fell asleep.

> "Only Noah was left, and those that were with him in the ark."
>
> *Genesis 7:23*

> "When these things begin to take place, look up and raise your heads...."
>
> *Luke 21:28*

> "Then a tremendous flash of light cut across the sky.... It seemed a sheet of sun."
>
> from *Hiroshima*, by John Hersey

CHAPTER ELEVEN

Thursday, October 25

"COME HOME AGAIN TODAY," my father said to me, rising from his breakfast. "We'll need you next week, but see what you can do here to help your Mom."

He leaned over to kiss my mother. They smiled, and he kissed her again, and he headed out of the kitchen. We soon heard his VW start, and he was off to the store.

I took *The New York Times* from under my father's coffee mug and studied the front page. The huge headline read:

SOME SOVIET SHIPS SAID TO VEER FROM CUBA; KHRUSHCHEV SUGGESTS A SUMMIT MEETING; THANT BIDS U.S. AND RUSSIA DESIST 2 WEEKS

The large photo at the top of the page showed Soviet ships bound for Cuba. The photograph was taken from the air. The caption explained: "Crates on deck of ship at bottom hold fuselages of Ilyshin-28 bombers, which have a 2,000 mile range, according to the department."

"Who would like to go out to buy pumpkins today?" my mother asked. "It's about time, and if you want to carve them when we get back...."

Beth and Danny were excited. Lynn said she would go.

"Tommy? Want to come?" my mother asked.

"No thanks. I'll be OK."

There were several articles about Cuba on page one. Some ships, I read, had altered their direction, while others were "still proceeding on course for Cuba." There was an article titled, "Homeowners Get Fallout Advice." I read most of it. One man recommended that families stock their basements well enough with food and water for ten days to two weeks. I wondered if that would be enough.

❦

I got off the bus that afternoon and ran up Bayberry Hill and across the front yard and reached the turnaround and saw that the trucks had already gone — and the shelter was buried. I waited until my mother had left with my brother and sisters before I went to work. I had a lot to do.

I found some boxes and brought them into the pantry to begin to pack. I filled one box with canned foods: many cans of Campbell's soup, canned beans, and some canned fruit.

Into a second box I added several cans of tuna fish, a box of Cheerios, Sugar Frosted Flakes, and Trix, two boxes of oreos and fig newtons, and a bag of marshmallows. Out of the cellar I took a flashlight and some batteries, and my father's radio. Back in the kitchen I filled three old milk gallons with water. I also remembered to go upstairs to my bathroom to get my toothbrush and toothpaste, and to get the first-aid kit and four rolls of toilet paper from the linen closet in the hallway. Then I carried out my first load.

I passed through the garden in the back yard, then stepped between the apple trees, and came to the huge patch of dirt. The only sign that something was beneath me were the pipes, and a metal hatchway. The two six-inch pipes, eight feet apart, almost came up to my knees. They weren't hollow, I noticed; later that evening my mother told me they contained filters, to keep out the radiation. Both pipes curled around at the top so that their opening was perpendicular to the ground; they looked strange — like two periscopes rising out of the sea, or two little "chimneys" for our underground house. The hatchway reminded me of the one Dorothy and Toto couldn't get into, in *The Wizard of Oz*, when the tornado came. Except that ours was red and shiny, not at all like that old wooden hatchway Dorothy had back in Kansas.

I lifted the right-hand side and then the left. The stairway was made of cement blocks. I counted: ten steps. It was awkward trying to climb down with the box in my arms, but I made it to the door. With a little jiggling the bar slid to the left, much more easily than it had on Wednesday, and the door opened. I stepped in, put the box down, and took a deep breath. It was musty and cold. It was even colder than it had been the day before. I would have to find some blankets.

I brought out the second box of foods, and on the third trip, after a long search through piles of clothes up in the attic, I filled my arms with blankets and sheets and four old pillows and lugged them outside. As I passed under one of the apples trees I tried to lift the blankets up high enough so that I could see where I was going and, if possible, avoid stepping on one of the many brown, mushy, worm-ridden apples still there. I heard something rustle through the leaves on the ground a few feet away, and I looked and saw a squirrel dart up the trunk and scramble out toward the end of a branch — right above me, less than ten feet over my head. I stopped. The squirrel stopped. I looked at it, frozen there, so near me — seven or eight feet away — shaking, quivering, struck dumb, it seemed, staring back at me. It held a small brown nut in its mouth. Its tail shivered. I almost felt I could hear a motor running inside its little body. I stared back, wondering at the incredible speed with which it shook, at the panic in its eyes, those eyes fixed on me. My load felt heavy, but I wanted to see if I could outlast him. "You flinch first," I thought, "and I win." We kept staring. Ten seconds. Fifteen seconds. But my left arm was aching. I shifted my weight — and the squirrel flew away, back to the trunk. I tried to follow it as it darted from branch to limb to branch, leaping from the tree above me and on to a second, scurrying ever higher, ever farther away, before coming to a rest, near the top of the apple tree closest to the garden.

I walked on into the bomb shelter, my heart still racing.

I went back inside for those three gallons of water. I wondered how many gallons Jody carried when he went off to the sink-hole and filled up those two wooden buckets....

"Ten days to two weeks," the paper had said that morning.

At least, I thought. Three gallons were just a start. But it was getting late. I wanted to have as much done as possible before my mother returned. This was my way of helping her, wasn't it? Even more important, though, I had to be done before my father came home.

One more trip, I decided. I checked the page of reminders from school; I was wearing the same khakis as the day before, and the list was still there in my hip pocket. Candles, fire extinguisher, gas stove. I ran inside and hurried through the house to collect all three. To get the gas stove I nearly had to crawl into the back of one of the pantry cabinets; as I was struggling to pull it out I heard my mother's car turn in the driveway.

Five minutes later I began to open the back door with my last load, and Lynn joined me just in time, holding the door, and picking up two sterno cans I dropped. She had a doll with her, as well as her own blanket.

"A fire extinguisher?" she asked, looking into my box.

I didn't understand it either.

"It's on the list they gave us," I said. I led her to the shelter, and I grabbed the flashlight and brought her down the steps. Once inside, she walked in a small circle. "Tiny, isn't it," she said, as if surprised. "What do we sleep on?"

I hadn't thought much about it.

"Blankets, I guess."

Then she checked the labels of the soup.

"Oh, great, clam chowder. Did you remember a can opener?" I shook my head. "That's OK. Now tomorrow we'll get a can opener, and some pots and pans and, well, bowls and plates and silverware—," and she took a deep breath, and added, "more pillows, and sleeping bags, or *something*. It's a lot." I kept the flashlight aimed at the wall to Lynn's left; it helped me see half of her face. She looked almost scary. Halloween. Maybe we would be here by Halloween.... Lynn grew silent, and began to twist the curls of her hair. Then she smoothed the hair of her doll and straightened the doll's body and lay her down on the blanket, as if for a nap. "Tommy," she said, taking a step closer to me, and almost whispering, "we'll be all right, won't we? Don't you think we'll be OK?"

I looked down at the radio and tried to get WABC in New York, at 77. It came in — not very strongly, but clearly enough. "Sherry," by The Four Seasons, was playing:

Sha-ar-ry, Sherry baby, Sha-ar-ry, Sherry baby,
Sha-a-a-a-er-ry bay-a-by, Sherry baby....

"I mean," she went on, "the kids at school who talk about it being the end of the world or something ... you don't believe that, do you?"

Come, come, come out toni-i-i-i-ight,
Come, come, come out toni-i-i-i-ight.

I turned the music down a little.

"Maybe," I began. "It's not impossible, you know. That's kind of why this is here. Because it's possible."

Lynn stood still. "But really Tommy, we can't live here forever."

Suddenly, though, her mood changed. "I know what we need. A mirror. And some paper." She seemed excited again. "Pens and paper, to write. We can keep a diary. And some games. Monopoly, Scrabble, cards, you know."

And *Sport* magazines, I thought. *The Yearling*.

"Hey, do you want to carve your pumpkin?" she said.
"No thanks," I said.
"OK, see you in a bit."

I tried to get a station where the music came in more loudly, without much luck. But the news was the main thing — only Lynn really needed to hear the music — and seven or eight stations sounded fine. I began to unpack and organize. We were camping out. We were going on a cruise. We were like Noah and his family, inside this ark, and the radio, the radio would be like the dove, telling us, "You can come out now. It's safe."

After twenty minutes I heard steps approach the shelter. My father's steps, by the heavy sound of them. I turned off the radio.

"Tommy, you in there?"

"Hi Dad," I answered, and walked to the door. He stood leaning over the opening, another seven or eight feet above me. The sky behind him was slightly darker now. But I could see his face quite well. He looked puzzled.

"What are you doing?"

"Do you want to see?" I asked.

He shook his head, no, and gave a sarcastic laugh, as if to say, "Of course not." Still, he came down. He put one foot on the first step and bounced on it. Then he turned his body around so that he descended facing the steps. I heard him mumble, "I suppose I must."

I gave him the flashlight. He stood and passed the light around the room for a while. He was breathing heavily; the air whistled through his nose. He went over to check the cans of food. From the doorway I watched him read their labels, slowly, tapping each can as he did so: "Hash, tuna, cream of mushroom, beef bullion, clam chowder, chicken and rice, tomato, corn, peas, baked beans...." He picked up some of the sterno cans. He saw my toothbrush, and picked it up, and began to turn, and then stopped and put it back down. He even picked up Lynn's doll. The wig fell off as he lifted it up. He bent over and took the wig — long brown hair with a firm curl to it, puffed out like Mrs. Kennedy's — and he stuck it back on, squeezing it against the doll's head tightly for ten seconds. Then he put the doll in a sitting position, with a quick snap, and returned her to Lynn's blanket.

He stepped away, into the middle of the room, and stood with his back to me for some time. By his silhouette, I imagined that he was looking at the soup cans. His shoulders lifted a little as he turned around. He pointed the flashlight down. He was staring at me — his jaw was looking my way, I could tell that — but I could not see his eyes. I knew he wasn't pleased. I wasn't sure if he was angry.

"I don't get it." He shook his head. "Tommy, I had no idea." He moved through the door, shutting off the flashlight as he did so, and putting it down by the first step. For a moment I thought he was going to climb out, and just leave me there. But he turned and sat on the edge of the third step. "Come here," he said. I stood in the doorway. It was getting dark out, and it was darker down there, at the bottom of those steps. My father reached out his arms and put his hands around my elbows. His eyes were almost even with mine.

"I hate to see you doing this boy." His voice was quiet. "You act as if this thing is bound to happen. It's not. I swear to God it's not," he said. "God knows you can't think like this. You can't live this way."

I gritted my teeth, and tried not to look away. Could I talk back to him? Could I let him know?

"Talk to me," he said.

And tell him — what? What he could not see for himself? That maybe we had no choice. That I didn't make all of this up. That it wasn't just in my imagination.

"If I learned nothing else last spring," he said, "when I had a hard time, I realized you can't keep it all in. Maybe you get this from me, Tommy, but please boy, don't bottle it all up inside."

But I could not find any words. I wanted to say something. I wanted him to understand. But how?

"Tommy, your mother loves all of you very much. That's why she wants this here, just in case. In case of a nuclear bomb. It's what she wants, and here it is, and so be it."

He grabbed me more tightly now, around the wrists.

"But son, please believe, we won't need this. We're going to be OK — and without this deathtrap here." His sandy hair looked dark, his blue eyes even darker. There was no anger in those eyes. But they told me he was hurt. And frustrated. And bewildered. I could hardly bear to look back. "I wish I could make you believe that."

I looked down. He could not make me believe that, I wanted to tell him, if I could have found the words. War and bombs — nuclear weapons — they all seemed very possible. My President had said they were possible. My school had said it, too. I did not understand much of what was happening, I knew that. I did not understand quarantines and surface-to-air missiles and national security, I did not understand atomic blasts and radiation and people melting, burning ... "burnt offerings." No, I did not understand.

And I did not understand why this might happen now, when I was only twelve years old.... I did not want this, he knew that, didn't he?

But wasn't I trying to be honest about it? Wasn't I trying to pay attention?

And wasn't I trying to help? What was I supposed to do? Nothing?

I kept my head down, and remained silent, and shrugged. I wanted this to be over. Please, Dad, I thought — no more.

His hands relaxed their grip and he gave me a pat on the shoulders. I raised my head.

"Come on," he said, beginning to get on his feet. "Let's go inside. I don't want to spend another minute here." And he turned and climbed the ten steps, and I followed.

I was relieved. He wasn't angry, not really. Disappointed in me, I thought — but not mad.

Besides, I had done much of what I had set out to do. Tomorrow I could finish. Tomorrow we would be ready.

My father closed the left door of the hatchway, then dropped the right door down, and it rang and echoed. He looked at me and put his right hand around my neck and rubbed it, hard.

"We'll be all right, we really will," he said.

And we walked under the apple trees, and through the garden, and into the house.

"Everything was in combat readiness on both sides. The conventional and nuclear forces of the United States were alerted worldwide. Both air-strike planes and the largest invasion force mounted since World War II were massed in Florida. Our little group seated around the Cabinet table in continuous session that Saturday felt nuclear war to be closer on that day than at any time in the nuclear age. If the Soviet ship continued coming, if the SAMs continued firing, if the missile crews continued working and if Khrushchev continued insisting on concessions with a gun at our head, then — we all believed — the Soviets must want a war and war would be unavoidable."

Theodore Sorensen
Kennedy

CHAPTER TWELVE

Thanksgiving

OVER THE NEXT FEW DAYS everything seemed quite normal. Again, there were no dramatic events, nothing that told the story there on TV — as happened over a year later, in November of 1963. We do not speak of "the tragic events" of the fall of 1962; dark days, maybe, tense moments ... but no, not a nation in shock, grieving together. We were asked to wait, and to imagine the possibilities, alone.

October 26

On Friday almost every article on the front page of the *Times* was about the crisis. A Russian tanker had been intercepted by the navy. Because it had no missiles on board, it was allowed to go through to Cuba. The huge photo across the top of the page was of Ambassador Stevenson, at the United Nations, showing photos of the missile bases in Cuba. Work on those missile sites, the paper said, was continuing. One headline read, **"Pope Bids Rulers Save the Peace."** Another story told me there were "potential fallout spaces for 60,000,000" Americans.

In first period I finally gave my talk on Berlin. Mr. Reynolds gave me a pat on the shoulder as I headed back to my desk, and said, "Good job, Chapman." I was glad to have it over, but less sure that I wanted his praise. "A crisis in Berlin, in their back yard, would be entirely different," Mr. Reynolds told us, as I took my seat. "And far more likely to create a nuclear threat. It's not like Cuba," he added, "sitting next door, where we have all the advantages."

We had another drill, in school, during the last period. Mr. Knapp seemed startled, too. I wondered if it was a drill, or the real thing. No one told me, or any of us, until it was over.

I continued to stock the shelter that afternoon. On one trip, as I brought out more gallons of water, my mother came with me. "I need to see what you've got out here," she said. She seemed amazed at how thorough I had been, but her simple, brief, "Thank you, Tommy," was far less than I had expected. She spent the next hour, though, working with Lynn and me. First she found an old mattress up in the attic, as well as six sleeping bags and several pillows, and we took them out to the shelter. Then she gathered more kitchen items. I filled up one box with the pots and pans and carried it out. Lynn followed with a second box, full of silverwear, plates, cups, coffee mugs, instant coffee, and ten more sterno cans for the stove. She left her box at the top step and shouted, "It's all yours!" I went back in to get the kerosene lamp and the three gallons of kerosene that my mother said we would need. She put them by the back door for me.

The shelves were quite full by the time I was done unpacking. Then I climbed back out and picked three dozen apples from the lower branches of the apple trees and brought them into the kitchen. My mother kept eight apples for a pie she was planning to make the next day; I washed all the others, quickly, as the clock told me it was 5:15. Then I took them out to the shelter. I was back in my room playing with Danny on his hockey set by 5:30.

October 27-28

My father asked me to work at the store that weekend, on Saturday morning. We raked and burned leaves both afternoons. In those piles not far from the shelter, apples that had fallen to the ground burned in the fires, too. I enjoyed that good, familiar smell of autumn. After completing the work, on both days, my father threw the football with Danny and me for over half an hour. And after lunch on Sunday the whole family played a game of touch football — my mother, Beth, and me against my father, Lynn, and Danny. As I was outside so much that weekend, I wondered how we would hear, so far away from the center of town, on Bayberry Hill. Those sirens at school were loud, but what could be loud enough to reach everyone in Riverdale? Was there some way of alerting all of us, the way those air-raid warnings told everyone in London that the German bombers were coming? And how quickly could it happen? Could it be as sudden as it was for those people in Hiroshima? Would some huge light explode to the west, over New York — and would we forget, and look? Who would warn us?

Several times each day I went out to the shelter to turn on the radio, in case we had missed something.

Saturday night my parents took all of us out to dinner and to a movie, "The Miracle Worker." For a while I felt uneasy being away from home. It was a twenty-minute drive back to Bayberry Hill. But once inside the theater, watching Helen Keller learn to speak, I forgot.

As I forgot, much of the time, while reading another forty pages of *The Yearling* that weekend.

Both mornings, however, I looked at the front page of *The New York Times* and read what I could. My father was still telling me, and all of us, not to worry. "They're working it out. Negotiations, cables, it takes time." The paper was less reassuring.

Saturday's headline read:

U.S. FINDS CUBA SPEEDING BUILD-UP OF BASES, WARNS OF FURTHER ACTION; U.N. TALKS OPEN; SOVIET AGREES TO SHUN BLOCKADE ZONE NOW

There were more photos of Ambassador Stevenson and Soviet diplomats at the top of the front page, and on the right, the smaller headline:

CAPITAL IS STERN

*Weighs Direct Steps
if Soviet Defiance
is Continued*

Sunday's headline read:

U.S. GETS SOVIET OFFER TO END CUBA BASES, REJECTS BID TO LINK IT TO THOSE IN TURKEY; U-2 LOST ON PATROL, OTHER CRAFT FIRED ON

I read of Secretary McNamara calling up twenty-four troop-carrier squadrons of the Air Force Reserve, about 14,000 men. Under the headline,

KENNEDY REPLIES

*Urges Kremlin Stand By
Initial Proposal*

Crisis Heightens

I read of letters going back and forth between Kennedy and Khrushchev. And I read of the threatened air strike of Cuba, if the Soviets did not stop.

There was a great deal I did not understand. But the main point remained clear: we were to be ready for "worldwide nuclear war." We would not "shrink from that risk." I could understand that.

I asked my father if he had talked with Uncle David. He said he had tried, several times, but had not been able to reach him.

There was an odd feeling in church that Sunday morning. It reminded me of my homeroom class, on Tuesday, after our first drill: as then, the church hall seemed unusually silent — and worried. I was astonished to hear the organist playing the tune of "My Country 'Tis of Thee" as I searched the red hymnal for the opening hymn; I couldn't remember singing this in church before. Reverend Marshall made sure that we prayed for President Kennedy and Premier Khrushchev, and for wisdom, and for peace. And then we said the Lord's Prayer together. "Thy kingdom come." Maybe it will, I remembered. Maybe soon.

After the Children's Sermon we prepared to head downstairs for Sunday School, singing the first verse of "God of our Fathers" with our parents. Then we dropped our hymnals and scurried into the aisles, walking — sometimes running — to the back doors. I caught up with Debbie. In class we discussed our chapter on Moses in Egypt — the plagues, the Passover, and the escape across the Red Sea. Death and survival. Miracles. God saving His people.

When did the crisis end? When did we celebrate the fact that no bombs were dropped, no one had to take shelter from the fallout — and we were safe?

I cannot remember any such moment. In fact, I had the feeling that the conflict between our two countries was still unresolved, was not quite over, for several more weeks.

For me, and perhaps for others, it never did come to a close. The confrontation endured. A collision — and the nightmare it could lead to — remained all too real a possibility, for much of our lives.

We learned later the crisis was ending that very Sunday morning, October 28. Kennedy accepted Khrushchev's pledge to withdraw the missiles from Cuba, under U.N. verification, in exchange for an end to the blockade and America's commitment not to invade Cuba. On Sunday evening my father called me in to watch the news. It sounded over. But how could they be sure? Even after reading Monday morning's top headline: **"U.S. & SOVIET REACH ACCORD ON CUBA,"** I still did not know what to feel. Could I stop worrying? What would Mr. Reynolds say?

But I walked in to Room 106 Monday morning and saw a woman at his desk, a substitute teacher, and soon learned that Mr. Reynolds was gone, was one of the reserves called up to active duty that weekend. His squadron was in Florida, we were told. He did not return until the middle of November.

Except for his absence, everything at school returned to normal within a few days. In homeroom we began to prepare for the December Fair. There were no more drills of that kind. Never again was I asked to practice for nuclear war. Soon after, and throughout our school years, more fallout shelter signs appeared — three orange upside-down triangles, inside a black circle, against an orange backdrop. We saw them all around us in school — in basements, and cafeterias, and hallways. They reminded us of that week in October of 1962. And of the possibility that the siren could sound once again, *"Nnnnn! Nnnnn! Nnnnn!"* ... But there were no more drills.

I remained unconvinced for another two or three weeks. By Thanksgiving I must have known it would not happen soon. Two days before Thanksgiving, on November 20, President Kennedy held a press conference. It was his first since September 13. He announced that the offensive missiles had all been loaded on Soviet ships, and that the Soviets had agreed to remove the remaining IL-28 bombers within thirty days. As a result, he was lifting the blockade. "May I add this final thought," the President said, "in this week of Thanksgiving: there is much for which we can be grateful as we look back to where we stood only four weeks ago...."

That weekend I brought most everything back inside — although the mattress stayed, and I kept some blankets there in the shelter, and the candles, the lamp, and a gallon of kerosene. The gallons of water stayed, too.

Still, there was no one moment when I could say: it is over. No one moment when I could say: there is no reason, any longer, to fear that we will have to hide — or worse — inside our shelter. To fear the bomb over New York, lighting up the sky. To fear the end.

"Besides, I may in fact get some relief from writing it all down. Today, for instance, I am particularly oppressed by a certain memory of long ago. It came to my mind vividly the other day, and ever since then it has stayed with me like an annoying tune that won't quite leave you alone."

Fyodor Dostoevsky
from *Notes from Underground* (translated by Mirra Ginsburg)

"Even hibernation can be overdone, come to think of it."

Ralph Ellison
from *Invisible Man*

EPILOGUE

I KEPT VISITING THE SHELTER, for the next two or three years. I learned how to use that kerosene lamp well. The shelter became a place to read — novels and sports magazines, mostly — and a place where I could do my homework, sometimes. And after I was given a GE transistor radio for my thirteenth birthday, it also became a place to listen to music. It was a place that was my own. Ian never liked it; he wouldn't camp out there with me, although Danny did, several nights. Most of the time, though, I went there by myself.

And the sad truth is, I stayed down there. Not literally, of course, but in some way, even after leaving home, long after my parents left Bayberry Hill and Riverdale, a part of me remained in that underground world, inside that protective shelter, unable to believe in the future. Long after I abandoned Mr. Saarinen's version of the last day, I continued to imagine that the end was near. U.S.-Soviet relations fluctuated, détente had its moments, but the worst always seemed possible. The number of warheads multiplied. Someday they would be used — accidentally or not. And we would blow ourselves up. It seemed logical, and inevitable. I wanted to believe something else, but could not. Or would not.

That I saw the world this way is not something I can entirely defend. After all, the calendar continued to turn ... past dates I was sure we would never see ... 1963, 1964, 1970, 1980, 1984, to the present.... And there were no moments quite like that week in October of 1962, the one time, historians agree, when we were close to the edge. The Cuban Missile Crisis was clearly an exception to the rule, right?

And time was passing. I was getting older. I held back from marriage, children, a future together. I held on to my fear — even if it cut me off, too much, from life. Couldn't I see there was little reason to insist on my doubts, to keep a part of myself buried down there, enclosed within those four walls? Why so stubborn? Why, especially in the light of so many blessings, so much to be grateful for?

Not long ago, without knowing when it had happened, I realized I had stepped out of that shelter. I looked around and realized I had been lifted out of that darkness, and I said, "We're going to be here. For some time to come." And it

Epilogue

made me glad. How much I owed to the fact that the Cold War was over, that World War III seemed almost inconceivable, and how much to more personal reasons, I can't say. I only know that I have regained a hope I once thought I had lost. I thank God, a less frightening God than the one I believed in that year, at twelve. And I thank my friends and family and everyone who helped me recover this hope. As Ellison's underground man put it, life, once again, is "full of possibilities."

※

The fall of 1974 was the first time I sat down and tried to recall the events of Tuesday, October 23 — the day Mrs. Brady asked us to prepare for nuclear war — in a short story. The narrative grew over the years; I left it, many times, but it "stayed with me," and kept after me. Dostoevsky's underground man wrote of the possibility of getting "some relief" by writing it all down. It surprises me, but yes, it *is* a relief to feel the story is told.

A relief I wouldn't have known, no doubt, if I had not been able to leave that shelter. If I had not come to believe that nuclear war — the doom I had so long imagined — would not take place.

Today, at last, I feel released from the doubts that sank into my heart that October, at twelve. A terror many of us have shared throughout the second half of this century.

True, not totally gone, not yet. This Cold War memory is about the past, but the weapons have not yet been put away. Darker possibilities still exist, and may throughout the rest of our lives. The proliferation of nuclear weapons; global arms trade and nuclear terrorism; efforts at arms control that creep along, with no sense of urgency.... There is much that needs to be done. There is good reason to be watchful.

But the dread of nuclear holocaust, the future we imagined and feared and grew up with — and the madness of it all — almost seems behind us.

Leaving us with other visions of the future to fear, no doubt.

But none as crippling.

Certainly none as deadly.

SHELTER – A Cold War Memory is available through your local bookstore or directly from the publisher.

>Shippen Press
>2395 S. Milwaukee St.
>Denver, CO 80210-5511
>(1-303-757-1225)

Book	*Shelter*	$7.95
Shipping	Regular Mail – first book	1.50
	Each additional book	.50
	Priority Mail – first book	3.00
	Each additional book	.50
Sales Tax	Outside Colorado	0
	Colorado (outside Metro Denver) add	.24
	Colorado, Metro Area (outside Denver) add	.30
	Denver add	.58

To Order   Please make check payable to Shippen Press. Phone orders accepted at 1-303-757-1225.

If you are interested in having the author read or speak to a group, contact Shippen Press.